Project for a Revolution
in New York

PROJECT FOR A REVOLUTION IN NEW YORK

A Novel by
Alain Robbe-Grillet

Translated from the French
by Richard Howard

Grove Press, Inc., New York

ISBN: 0-394-17768-1
Grove Press ISBN: 0-8021-4036-X

Library of Congress Catalog Card Number: 77-187581

First Evergreen Edition 1976

Third Printing 1978

Manufactured in the United States of America

Distributed by Random House, Inc., New York

GROVE PRESS, INC., 196 West Houston Street,
New York, N.Y. 10014

Project for a Revolution in New York

The first scene goes very fast. Evidently it has already been rehearsed several times: everyone knows his part by heart. Words and gestures follow each other in a relaxed, continuous manner, the links as imperceptible as the necessary elements of some properly lubricated machinery.

Then there is a gap, a blank space, a pause of indeterminate length during which nothing happens, not even the anticipation of what will come next.

And suddenly the action resumes, without warning, and the same scene occurs again . . . But which scene? I am closing the door behind me, a heavy wooden door with a tiny narrow oblong window near the top, its pane protected by a cast-iron grille (clumsily imitating wrought iron) which almost entirely covers it. The interlacing spirals, thickened by successive layers of black paint, are so close together, and there is so little light from the other side of the door, that nothing can be seen of what might or might not be inside.

The wood around the window is coated with a brownish varnish in which thin lines of a lighter color, lines which are the imitation of imaginary veins running through another substance considered more decorative, constitute parallel networks or networks of only slightly divergent curves outlining darker knots, round or oval or even triangular, a group of changing signs in which I have discerned human figures for a long time: a young woman lying on her left side and facing me, apparently naked since her nipples and pubic hair are discernible; her legs are bent, the left one more than the right, its knee pointing forward, on the floor; the right foot therefore crosses over the left one, the ankles are evidently bound together, just as the wrists are bound behind her back as usual, it would seem, for both arms disappear from view behind the upper part of the body: the left arm below the elbow and the right one just above it.

The face, tilted back, is framed by curling waves of very dark, luxuriant hair spread loose on the tiles. The features themselves are difficult to make out, as much because of the position of the head as because of a broad hank of hair slanting across the forehead, the line of the eyes, and one cheek: the only indisputable detail is the mouth, open in a long cry of suffering or terror. From the left part of the frame spreads a cone of harsh light, emanating from a lamp with a jointed arm whose base is clamped to the corner of a metal desk; the shaft of light has been carefully directed, as though for an interrogation, toward the harmonious curves of amber flesh lying on the floor.

Yet it cannot be an interrogation; the mouth, which has been wide open too long, must be distended by some kind of gag: for example, a piece of black lingerie stuffed between the lips. Besides, a scream, if the girl were screaming, would be audible even through the thick pane of the oblong window with its cast-iron grille.

But now a silver-haired man in a white doctor's

coat appears in the foreground from the right; he is seen from behind, so that only a hint of his face can be glimpsed in profile. He walks toward the bound girl whom he stares at for a moment, standing over her, his own body concealing a part of her legs. The captive must be unconscious, for she does not react to his approach; moreover, a closer look at the gag's shape and arrangement just under the girl's nose reveals that it is a wad of cloth soaked in ether which was necessary to overcome the resistance indicated by the disheveled hair.

The doctor bends forward, kneels down on one knee and begins to untie the cords binding her ankles. The girl's body, docile now, lies prostrate as two steady hands part the knees, spreading the smooth brown thighs which glisten in the lamplight; but the upper part of the body does not lie flat because of the arms which remain bound together behind the back; the breasts, in this change of position, are merely easier to see: firm as two foam-rubber domes and splendidly proportioned, they are slightly paler than the rest of the body, their lovely sepia aureoles (which are not very large, for a half-caste girl) swelling a little around the nipples.

After getting up a moment and taking from the metal desk a sharp-pointed instrument about a foot long, the doctor has resumed his kneeling position, but a little farther to the right, so that his white coat now conceals the upper part of the girl's thighs. The man's hands, invisible for the moment, are performing some operation in the pubic region, though its exact nature is difficult to determine. Granted that the patient has been anesthetized, it can scarcely be a question, in any case, of some torture inflicted by a madman upon a victim chosen for her beauty alone. There remains the possibility of an artificial insemination effected by force (the object the surgeon is holding would then be a catheter) or of some other medical experiment of monstrous nature, performed of course without the subject's consent.

What the person in the white coat was going to do to his captive will never be known, unfortunately, for at this moment the rear door opens quickly and a third figure appears: a tall man who stands motionless in the doorway. He is wearing a tuxedo and his face and head are entirely hidden by a thin soot-colored leather mask with only five openings: a slit for the mouth, two tiny round orifices for the nostrils and two larger ovals for the eyes. These remain fixed on the doctor, who slowly straightens up and begins backing toward the other door, while behind the masked figure appears another one: a short bald man in workman's clothes with the strap of a toolbox over one shoulder, apparently a plumber, or an electrician, or a locksmith. The whole scene then goes very fast, still without variation.

It has obviously been rehearsed several times: everyone knows his part by heart. The gestures follow each other in a relaxed, continuous manner, the links as imperceptible as the necessary elements of some properly oiled machinery, when suddenly the light goes out. The only thing left in front of me is a dusty pane in which no more than a dim reflection of my own face can be made out, and the housefront behind me, between the interlacing spirals of the heavy black ironwork. The surface of the wood around it is coated with a brownish varnish in which thin lines of a lighter color are supposed to represent the grain of the oak. The bolt falls into place with a muffled click, prolonged by a cavernous echo which spreads through the entire mass of the door, immediately dying out into complete silence.

I release the bronze doorknob shaped like a hand holding a skewer or stylus or slender dagger in its sheath, and I turn all the way around to face the street, about to descend the three imitation-stone steps between the threshold and the sidewalk, its asphalt glistening now after the rain, people hurrying by in hopes of reaching home before the next shower, before their delay (they must have waited somewhere a long while) causes alarm, before dinner time, before nightfall.

The click of the lock has set off the customary mechanism: I have forgotten my key inside and I can no longer open the door to get it back. This is not true, of course, but the image is still as powerful of the tiny steel key lying on the right-hand corner of the marble table top near the brass candlestick. So there must be a table in this dim vestibule.

It is a dark piece of furniture, its mahogany veneer in poor condition, which must date from the second half of the preceding century. On the dull black marble, the little key stands out with all the clarity of a primer illustration. Its flat, perfectly round ring lies only a couple of inches from the hexagonal base of the candlestick, etc., whose ornamental shaft (fillets, tori, cavettos, cymae, scotias, etc.) supports . . . etc. The yellow brass glistens in the dark, on the right side where a faint light filters through the grille covering the window in the door.

Above the table a large oblong mirror is hanging on the wall, tilted slightly forward. Its wooden frame, the gilding faded on the unidentifiable carved leaves, delimits a misty surface with the bluish depths of an aquarium, the central part occupied by the half-open library door and an uncertain, fragile, remote figure—it is Laura standing motionless on the other side of the threshold.

"You're late," she says. "I was beginning to worry."

"I had to wait until the rain stopped."

"Was it raining?"

"Yes, a long while."

"Not here . . . And you're not even wet."

"No—because I waited."

My hand releases the little key I had just set down on the marble when I glanced up toward the mirror. Memory of the contact with the already cooled metal (which my palm had warmed a moment before) still remains on the sensitive skin of my finger tips as I turn all the way around to face the street, immediately starting down the three imitation-stone steps leading from the door to the sidewalk. With a habitual gesture—futile, insistent, inevitable—I check to discover whether the little steel key is in the usual pocket where I have just slipped it. At this moment I notice the man in black—shiny raincoat with the collar turned up, hands in his pockets, soft felt hat low over his eyes—waiting on the opposite sidewalk.

Though he appears to be more concerned to avoid notice than the rain, his motionless figure immediately attracts attention among the people hurrying past after the shower. Moreover, they are less numerous now, and the man, feeling exposed, gradually draws back into the recess afforded by one housefront

—that of number 789 A, whose stucco is painted bright blue.

This house has three stories, like all its neighbors (which constitute, about a yard closer to the curb, the general alignment of the street), but it must be of more recent construction, for it is the only one without a fire escape: a skeleton of black intersecting lines form superimpozed Z's on the façade of each apartment building and end about ten feet from the ground. A thin removable ladder, usually raised, offers means to reach the sidewalk and permit escape from the fire blazing on the stairs inside.

A skillful burglar, or a murderer, could catch hold of the lowest rung, hoist himself up, and then simply climb the metal steps to the French window of any floor and enter the room he chooses, merely by breaking a single pane. At least this is what Laura imagines. The sound of the broken pane, whose splinters tinkle on the floor at the end of the corridor, has awakened her with a start.

She remains sitting bolt upright in her bed, motionless, holding her breath, not turning on the light in order to conceal her presence from the criminal who, having carefully thrust his hand between the sharp points of glass into the hole he has just poked with his revolver barrel or its heavier cross-hatched butt, or with the ivory handle of his switchblade, is now opening the window latch without making a sound. The harsh light of a nearby streetlamp casts its even larger shadow across the bright housefront, above the distorted shadow of the fire escape, whose various networks of parallel rays cross-hatch the whole surface of the building in a precise and complicated pattern.

7

When I open the bedroom door, I find Laura in this same posture of anxious expectation: sitting up in bed, leaning back against the bolster on both arms, head raised. The light from the corridor, where I have pressed the switch in passing, gleams in the dark room on the young woman's blond hair, pale flesh, and nightgown. She must have been asleep, for the material of the nightgown is rumpled into countless creases.

"It's you," she says. "You're so late. You frightened me."

Standing on the threshold of the wide-open doorway, I answer that the meeting lasted longer than usual.

"Nothing new?" she asks.

"No," I say, "nothing new."

"Did you drop something on your way upstairs?"

"No. Why? And I walked as softly as I could . . . Did you hear anything special?"

"It sounded like broken glass on the tiles . . ."

"Maybe it was my keys, when I set them down on the marble."

"Downstairs? No, it was much closer . . . Just at the end of the corridor."

"No," I say, "you were dreaming."

I step into the room. Laura leans back, but she is not completely relaxed. She stares up at the ceiling, eyes wide, as if she were still hearing suspicious creaks, or as if she were trying to remember something. After a pause she asks, "What's it like outside?"

"It's a quiet night."

Her transparent nightgown reveals the dark nipples of her breasts.

"I'd like to go out," she says, without looking at me.

"You would? Where?"

"Nowhere. Out into the street . . ."

"At this time of night?"

"Yes."

"You can't."

"Why not?"

"You can't . . . It's raining."

I would rather not mention to her now the man in the black raincoat waiting in front of the house, on the sidewalk across the street. I start to close the door, but just at that moment, even before my hand has reached the edge of the door which I am about to push back, the light goes off in the corridor, and my silhouette, dark against the lighted doorway, immediately vanishes.

Made threatening perhaps by the raised arm, the extent of the movement, the muffled impact of the fist against the wood in the sudden darkness, the half-glimpsed image has alarmed the young woman, who utters a faint moan. She then hears, on the thick carpeting which covers the entire floor of the room, the heavy footsteps coming closer to her bed. She tries to scream, but a firm warm hand presses against her mouth, while she feels the sensation of a crushing mass which slides toward her and soon overwhelms her altogether.

With his other hand, the aggressor roughly crumples the nightgown as he pulls it up, in order to immobilize the supple body still trying to struggle, grasping the flesh itself. The young woman thinks of the door, which has remained wide open to the empty corridor. But she does not manage to articulate a single sound. And it is a husky, threatening voice which murmurs near her ear, "Keep still, you little fool, or I'll hurt you."

The man is much stronger than this frail young creature whose resistance is fruitless, trifling, and absurd. With a quick movement he has released her mouth to grab both wrists and pull them behind her, imprisoning them in one hand now in the hollow of her back, so that her hips are arched. And immediately, with the other hand and the help of his knees, he brutally parts her thighs which he then caresses more gently, as though to tame some wild animal. The young woman feels at the same time the contact of the rough material (is it a wool sweater?) which presses harder against her belly and breasts.

Her heart is pounding so loud that she has the sense it can be heard all through the house. With a slow, imperceptible movement, she shifts her shoulders and hips slightly, in order to make her fetters more comfortable and her position more accessible. She has given up the struggle.

"And then?"

Then she gradually calmed down. She stirred a little once again, apparently trying to release her aching arms, but without conviction, as though merely to make sure such a thing was impossible. She whispered two or three inaudible words and her head suddenly fell to one side; then she began moaning again, more softly; but not in terror—not only in terror, in any case. Her blond hair, whose curls are still glistening in the darkness, as if they were phosphorescent, has rolled to the other side and, drowning the invisible face, sweeps the bolster from right and left, alternately, faster and faster, until long successive spasms run through her entire body.

When she seemed dead, I released my grip. I undressed very fast and came back to her. Her flesh was warm and sweet, her limbs were quite limp, the joints obedient; she had become as malleable as a rag doll.

Again I had that impression of tremendous fatigue which I had already experienced on my way upstairs a moment before. Laura fell asleep at once in my arms.

"Why is she so nervous? You know that means an extra danger—for no reason."

"No," I say, "she doesn't seem abnormally nervous . . . After all, she's very young . . . But she'll be all right. We're going through a rather hard time."

Then I tell him about the man in the black raincoat keeping watch on my door. He asks me if I'm sure I'm the person being watched. I answer no—I don't think it's me, in fact. Then he asks me, after a pause, if there's someone else to be shadowed in the neighborhood. I answer that I wouldn't know, but that there could be someone without my having any idea of it.

Tonight, when I left, the man was in his usual place, still in the same clothes and the same position: his hands deep in his raincoat pockets, his feet wide apart. There was no one near him, now, and his entire attitude, so assertive in his clothes—like a man on sentry duty—was so completely lacking in discretion that I wondered if he was really trying to avoid notice.

I had scarcely closed the door behind me when I saw the two policemen coming toward us. They were wearing the flat caps of the tactical police, the front edge very high, with the shield beneath and a broad shiny visor. They were walking in step, as though on

11

patrol, right down the middle of the street. My first impulse was to reopen my door and get back inside until the danger was past, observing from behind the little grille the sequence of events. But then I thought that it was absurd to hide so obviously. Moreover, the gesture I made toward the key in my pocket could only be that belated mechanical precaution I have already mentioned.

I calmly walked down the three stone steps. The man in the raincoat had not yet noticed—apparently —the presence of the tactical police, which seemed strange to me. Though they were still about two blocks away, you could hear the regular noise of their boots on the pavement quite distinctly. There was not one car in the street, which was deserted except for these four people: the two policemen, the motionless man, and myself.

Hesitating a second between the two possible directions, I thought first that it would be better to take the same direction as the policemen and to turn at the first intersection, before they could have seen my fact at close range. As a matter of fact it is very doubtful that they would have marched any faster, without a specific reason, in order to catch up with me. But after three steps in that direction, I decided that it would be better to face the ordeal directly, rather than to draw attention to myself by behavior which might seem suspicious. So I turned around in order to walk along the housefronts in the other direction, toward the policemen who were continuing their steady, straight march. On the opposite sidewalk, the man in the felt hat was staring at me calmly, as though with complete indifference: because there was nothing else to look at.

I walked on, looking straight ahead of me. The two policemen had no particular character: they were wearing the usual navy-blue jacket and leather belt and shoulder strap, with the pistol holster on one hip. They were of the same height—quite tall—and had rather similar faces: frozen, watchful, vacant. As I passed them, I did not turn my head toward them.

But, a few yards farther on, I wanted to know how the meeting with the other man would turn out, and I glanced back. The man in the black raincoat had finally noticed the policemen (probably when they were between him and me, in the line of his gaze, which was still fixed on me), and he made, just at that moment, a gesture with his right hand toward the turned-down brim of his hat . . .

There wasn't even time for me to wonder about the meaning of this gesture. The two policemen, quite unpredictably, with one accord turned around to stare at me, freezing me where I stood.

I can't say what they did next, for I immediately went on walking, with an instinctive about-face whose abruptness I immediately regretted. Moreover, hadn't my entire behavior since the beginning of the scene given me away: a hesitation (and doubtless a movement of withdrawal) on the threshold upon noticing the policemen, then an unaccountable change of direction which betrayed the initial intention of running away, finally an excessive stiffness at the moment of passing the patrol, whereas it would have been more natural to glance as though by chance at the two men, especially if I was to turn around to look at them subsequently as they walked away from me. All of which, obviously, justified their suspicions and their desire to see what this individual was up to behind their backs.

But what was the relation between this understandable suspicion and the gesture made by the other man? That almost looked like a tiny salute: the hand, which till then had never left the raincoat pocket, suddenly appearing and rising casually to the indented brim of the soft hat. It is difficult in any case to suppose that it was the intention of this placid sentry to lower the felt any farther over his eyes in order to conceal his face from the policemen altogether . . . Instead, doesn't the hand emerging from the pocket and slowly rising point to the man walking away, wanted by the inspectors for several days and whose suspicious behavior has yet again aggravated the already heavy charges weighing upon him?

However, he continues on his way nonetheless, walking faster in fact, while trying not to let this be too apparent to the three witnesses behind him: in front of the building painted bright blue, the two policemen are still frozen like statues, their expressionless gaze fixed on this receding figure, soon tiny at the end of the long straight street, while the gloved hand of the man in black, completing a slow trajectory, has just come to rest against the far edge of the felt hat.

Over there, as if he imagined he was henceforth out of sight, the suspect person begins going down the invisible staircase of a subway entrance which is in front of him, level with the ground, thereby losing successively his legs, his torso and his arms, his shoulders, his neck, his head.

Laura, behind the window corresponding to the third-floor corridor, at the very top of the fire escape, looks down at the long street, at this hour quite abandoned, thus making the three disturbing presences all the more remarkable. The man in black whom she has already noticed the last few days (how many?) is at his post, as she suspected he would be, in his usual shiny raincoat. But two policemen in flat caps, wearing high boots and pistol holsters, walking side by side down the middle of the pavement, have also stopped now a few steps from the first observer—who gestures to them with one hand—and turn around in unison to look at what he is pointing at: the window where Laura is standing.

She quickly steps back, quickly enough for neither the policemen nor their informant to be able to complete their head-movements upward before she herself has vanished from the place indicated by the black-gloved hand. But her recoil has been so rapid and spontaneous that it is accompanied by a clumsy gesture of her left hand, on which the heavy silver ring has just knocked violently against the pane.

The impact has produced a loud, distinct noise. At the same time has appeared, extending across the entire surface of the rectangle, a star-shaped fracture. But no piece of glass falls out, unless, much later, it is a tiny pointed triangle, about half an inch long, which slowly leans inward and falls on the tiles with a crystalline sound, breaking in its turn into three smaller fragments.

Laura stares a long time at the broken pane, then through the next one, which is similar but intact, at the blue wall of the house on the other side of the street, then at the three tiny splinters of glass scattered on the floor, and again at the starred pane. From the withdrawn position she now occupies in the corridor, she no longer sees the entire street. She wonders if the men watching her have heard the noise of glass breaking and if they can see the hole she has just made in the pane located below and to the left of the iron latch. To be sure, she would have to put her eye to that hole, leaning down to get closer to the window and then gradually raising her face against the pane of glass.

But the lower pane itself may not be hidden from view—may be visible to the man in the black raincoat and soft felt hat—because of the landing of the fire escape, actually a discontinuous structure consisting of parallel strips of iron which are not contiguous and leave openings between them of an equal width through which can be seen, from either side . . . From this side—that is, from up above, looking down —doubtless more easily, for the metal platform in question is much closer to the window than to the ground. The fact remains nonetheless that the straight line connecting the lower pane to the indented brim of the felt hat may run well above it; and this would be all the more true of the broken pane.

Once again the young woman remembers that her brother has forbidden her, under threat of severe punishment, to show herself at the windows overlooking the street—her brother who must have left the house just when the policemen had reached the neighborhood: she did not see him go out or walk away, but, when he leaves, he stays on the near sidewalk anyway, entirely invisible from the closed window, even to someone who stands right next to the pane.

He may also not yet have gone outside, having had time in the vestibule to realize the danger, inspecting the situation through the opening protected by a grille set in the wood of the door. And he is still, at this very moment, at his concealed observation post, wondering why the three policemen are looking up that way, unless he has immediately understood the reason, having himself heard, from downstairs, the sound of the broken pane which has drawn their attention to the third floor.

And now he is silently coming back upstairs to catch the disobedient girl red-handed: creeping up to a windowpane exposed to all eyes, and this moreover at precisely the moment when the justification for the prohibition is particularly obvious.

After having laid his key as usual on the marble table top, near the brass candlestick, he slowly mounts the steps, one by one, leaning on the wooden banister, for the excessive steepness of the stairs makes him feel once more the accumulated fatigue of the last several days: several days of watchfulness, expectation, of prolonged meetings, of errands by subway or on foot from one end of the city to the other, as far as the most outlying districts, far beyond the river . . . For how many days?

Having reached the first landing, he stops in order to listen, ears cocked for the faint creaks throughout the building. But there is neither a creak, nor the sound of material tearing, nor breath caught; there is nothing but silence and closed doors along the empty corridor.

He resumes his ascent. Laura, who had knelt on the terra cotta tiles and was beginning to crawl toward the window, in order to see what was happening outside now, suddenly frightened, turns around and sees, only a yard above her face, the man leaning over her whom she has not heard coming, but who suddenly overwhelms her with his motionless and threatening bulk. With the reflex of a child found out, she quickly raises one elbow to protect her face (although he has not made the least gesture of violence toward her) and, attempting at the same time to draw back in order to avoid being slapped, she slips, loses her balance, and sprawls back on the floor, one leg stretched out, the other bent beneath her, the upper part of her body supported on one elbow, the other still crooked in a traditional attitude of frightened defense.

She looks extremely young: perhaps sixteen or seventeen. Her hair is startlingly blond; the loose curls frame her pretty, terrified face with many golden highlights caught in the bright illumination from the window, against which she is silhouetted. Her long legs are revealed as far as the upper part of the thighs, the already short skirt being raised still farther in her fall, which exposes and emphasizes their lovely shape almost up to the pubic region, which can in fact be discerned in the shadows under the raised hem of the material.

Aside from the attitude of the two figures (which indicates both the rapidity of the movement and the violent tension of its suspension) the scene includes an objective trace of struggle: a broken pane whose splinters lie scattered on the regular hexagons of the tiles. The girl moreover has injured her hand, either because she has scraped it on the broken pane as she fell or because she has cut it a few seconds later on the glass splinters lying on the floor, or because she herself has broken the pane in her fall when the man brutally pushed her against the window, unless of course she acted deliberately: breaking the pane with her fist in the hopes of obtaining a glass dagger, as a defensive weapon against an aggressor.

A little bright-red blood, in any case, stains the hollow of her raised palm, and also, upon closer inspection, one of her knees, the one which is bent. This vermilion color is precisely the same as the one which covers her lips, as well as the very small surface of skirt visible in the picture. Above, the young girl is wearing a thin powder-blue garment which clings to her young bosom, a blouse of some shiny material whose neckline seems however to be torn. No earrings, nor necklace, nor bracelet, nor wedding ring is shown, only the left hand wears a heavy silver ring, drawn so carefully that it must play an important part in the story.

The bright-colored poster is reproduced several dozen times, pasted side by side all along the subway passageway. The play's title is *The Blood of Dreams*. The male character is a Negro. Till now I have never heard of this show, doubtless a recent one which has not been reviewed in the papers. As for the names of the performers, printed moreover in very tiny letters, they seem quite unknown to me. It is the first time I have seen this advertisement, in the subway or elsewhere.

Deciding that my pause has lasted long enough now to give any possible pursuers the chance to catch up with me, I turn around again and once again observe that no one is following me. The long corridor, from one end to the other, is empty and silent, very dirty like all the rest on this subway line, strewn with various papers, from torn newspapers to candy wrappers, and marked by more or less disgusting damp stains.

The brand-new poster which stretches as far as the eye can see, in either direction, also contrasts by its brightness with the remainder of the walls, covered with a ceramic tile which must originally have been white but whose surface is now cracked, chipped, stained with brownish streaks, broken at certain points as though someone had pounded it with a hammer.

At the other end, the corridor opens onto a huge similarly deserted area, an enormous underground hall with no apparent function, in which nothing can be made out that suggests—neither architectural detail nor signboard—any particular direction to follow; unless placards are mounted on certain surfaces but these are so remote, given the considerable dimensions of the place, and its dim illumination, that nothing identifiable is apparent in any direction, the very limits of this useless and vacant interval being lost in the uncertainty of the zones of shadow.

The very low ceiling is supported by countless hollow metal beams, whose four sides are perforated with floral patterns dating from an earlier period. These pillars are quite close together, only about five or six feet apart, set regularly in parallel lines, which divides the entire area into equal and contiguous squares. The checkerboard is moreover materialized on the ceiling by identical rafters jointing the capitals in pairs.

Suddenly the asphalt floor is interrupted, for a considerable length, by a series of stairways with alternating railings, ascending and descending, each of whose first step occupies the entire distance between two ironwork pillars. The whole seems conceived for the flow of a huge crowd which obviously no longer exists in any case at this hour. In two opposing flights, a lower area is reached, resembling the upper one in every particular. On a still lower level, I finally reached the shopping gallery, brilliantly illuminated this time by many-colored harsh bulbs, the more painful to the eyes in that the upper areas were only dimly lit.

And with a similar lack of transition, there is also a crowd now: a rather scattered crowd, but one of regular density, consisting of isolated figures or those grouped by two or, exceptionally, three, occupying the whole of the surface accessible between the stalls as well as that inside them. Here there are only young people, mostly boys, although a close examination reveals among some of these, under the short hair, tight blue jeans, and turtle-neck sweaters or leather jackets, probable or even incontestable girls' bodies. All are dressed alike, but their beardless pink and blond faces also look alike, with that bright and uninflected coloration which suggests not so much good health as the paint used on store-window mannequins, or the embalmed faces of corpses in glass coffins in the cemeteries of the dear departed. The impression of artificiality is further enhanced by the awkward postures of these young people, doubtless intended to express self-confidence, controlled strength, scorn, arrogance, whereas their stiff attitudes and the ostentation with which every gesture is made actually suggest the constraint of poor actors.

Among them, on the contrary, like tired guards in a wax museum, linger here and there occasional adults of indeterminate age, discreet and inconspicuous as if they were trying not to be seen; and as a matter of fact, it takes a certain amount of time to become aware of their presence. They reveal in their gray faces, their drawn features, their uncertain movements, the quite visible signs of the night hour, already very late. The livid glare of the neon tubes completes the illusion of invalids or addicts; the various races have here become almost the same metallic tinge. The huge greenish mirror of a store window reflects my own quite comparable image.

Nonetheless, old and young possess one characteristic in common, which is the excessive slackening of every movement, whose affected deliberation among some, whose extreme lethargy among others, threaten at any moment a total and definitive breakdown. And all this is, moreover, remarkably silent: neither shouts nor words spoken too loud, nor racket of any kind manages to disturb the muffled, padded atmosphere, broken only by the clicking of slot-machine levers and the dry crackling or clatter of scores automatically registered.

For this underground area seems entirely devoted to amusements: on each side of the huge central mall open out huge bays filled with long rows of the gleaming garish-painted devices: slot machines whose enigmatic apertures, which respectively devour and spit forth change, are embellished so as to make more obvious their resemblance to the female organ, games of chance allowing the player to lose in ten seconds some hundreds of thousands of imaginary dollars, automatic distributors of educational photographs showing scenes of war or copulation, pinball machines whose scoreboards include a series of villas and limousines, in which fires break out as a result of the movements made by the steel balls, shooting galleries with tracer bullets trained on the pedestrians in an avenue set up as the target, dartboards representing the naked body of a pretty girl crucified against a stake, racing cars driven by remote control, electric baseball, stereopticons of horror films, etc.

There are also, alongside, huge souvenir shops in which are set out, arranged in parallel rows of identical objects, plastic reproductions of world capitals and famous structures, ranging, from top to bottom of the display, from the Statue of Liberty, the Chicago stockyards, to the giant Buddha of Kamakura, the Blue Villa in Hong Kong, the lighthouse at Alexandria, Christopher Columbus' egg, the Venus of Milo, Greuze's *Broken Pitcher*, the Eye of God carved in marble, Niagara Falls with its wreaths of mist made out of iridescent nylon. Lastly there are the pornographic bookshops, which are merely the extension in depth of those of Forty-Second Street, a few yards, or dozen of yards, or hundreds of yards up above.

I discover without difficulty the shop window I want, easily found because it displays nothing: it is a wide plain ground-glass sheet with the simple inscription in moderate-sized enamel letters: "Dr. Morgan, Psychotherapist." I turn the nearly invisible handle of a door made of the same ground glass, and I step into a very small bare cubicle, all six surfaces painted white (in other words, the floor as well), in which are only a tubular-steel chair, a matching table with an artificial marble top on which is lying a closed engagement book whose black imitation-leather cover shows the date "1969" stamped in gold letters, and behind this table, sitting very stiffly on a chair identical with the first, a blond young woman—quite pretty perhaps, impersonal and sophisticated in any case, wearing a dazzlingly white nurse's uniform, her eyes concealed by sunglasses which doubtless help her endure the intense lighting, white like everything else and reflected on all sides by the immaculate walls.

She looks at me without speaking. The lenses of her sunglasses are so dark that it is impossible to guess even the shape of her eyes. I bring myself to pronounce the sentence, carefully separating the words as if each of them contained an isolated meaning: "I've come for a narco-analysis."

After a few seconds thought, she gives me the anticipated reply, but in an oddly natural voice, gay and spontaneous, suddenly bursting out: "Yes . . . It's quite late . . . What's the weather like outside right now?" And her face immediately freezes again, while her body has regained its mannequin stiffness at the same time. But I answer right back, still in the same neutral tone, insisting on each syllable: "It's raining outside. People are walking with their heads bent under the rain."

"All right," she says (and suddenly there is a kind of weariness in her voice), "are you a regular patient or is this your first visit?"

"This is my first visit here."

Then after having looked at me again for a moment—at least so it seems to me—through her dark glasses, the young woman stands up, walks around the table and, though the narrowness of the room does not at all require her to do so, brushes against me so insistently that her perfume clings to my clothes; in passing she points to the empty chair, continues to the far wall, turns around and says to me: "Sit down."

And she has immediately vanished, through a door so well concealed in the white partition that I had not even noticed its glass knob. The continuity of the surface is re-established, moreover, so quickly that I could now suspect I never saw it broken. I have just sat down when, through the opposite door opening onto the shopping mall, walks one of the men with iron-gray faces I glimpsed a few minutes earlier standing in front of a bookshop window: his body was turned toward the row of specialized magazines and papers on display, but he kept glancing right and left, as if he was afraid of being watched, though at times his eyes rested with some deliberation on an expensive magazine of which an entire row of identical copies were displayed at eye level, showing on its cover the full-color photograph, life size, of an open vagina.

Now he is looking at me, then at the table and the empty chair behind it. Finally he brings himself to pronounce the sentence: "I've come for a narco-analysis." Without omitting or changing a single word, I could give him the right answer, but it does not seem to me to be my part to do so; therefore I speak no more than the beginning, in order to reassure him even so: "Yes . . . It's quite late." Then I improvise: "The doctor's assistant has gone out. But I think she'll be right back."

"Oh good. Thank you," the gray-faced man says, turning toward the ground-glass window opening onto the mall, exactly as if he could see through it and had chosen this sight as a diversion, to help pass the time.

Suddenly I am filled with suspicion as I notice the way in which the newcomer is dressed: shiny black raincoat and soft felt hat with the brim turned down . . . Unless his back merely reminds me of the disturbing figure I have just seen pressed up against the display of the pornographic bookstore . . . But now the

25

man, as though to give more consistency to the disturbing connection I cannot help making, straightening up in his raincoat, thrusts his black-gloved hands deep into its broad pockets.

Without leaving me time to wait for the man to show his face again, so that I might recognize what he looks like even when his features are drawn by fatigue, the young woman in the nurse's uniform returns and very quickly gets rid of me. According to her directions, I leave through the rear door with the glass knob and climb a steep narrow spiral staircase made of cast iron.

Then there is a long corridor entirely covered (except for the floor) with that dilapidated white ceramic tile already described during the passage through the subway station, in which, as a matter of fact, I must still be walking. At the end of the hallway, a tiny sliding door with an electric-eye device opens automatically to let me through, and finally I enter the room where, if I have understood correctly, we are to be given our orders for tomorrow. Here there are some fifty persons. I immediately wonder how many police informers there can already be among them. Since I have come in at the rear of the room, I see the people in it only from the back, which does not make any such estimate easy—in fact, ridiculous.

I imagined I was ahead of time; it appears on the contrary that the meeting has already been going on for some time. And it is not concerned with the usual specific details, concerning imminent action. Instead, today, the meeting is given over to a kind of ideological discussion presented in the usual form, whose didactic effectiveness on the militants of every persuasion has been readily acknowledged: a prefabricated dialogue between or among three persons assigned alternately questions and answers, changing parts by a circular permutation at each shift of the text—i.e., about every minute.

The sentences are short and simple—subject, verb, complement—with constant repetitions and antitheses, but the vocabulary includes quite a large number of technical terms belonging to various fields, philosophy, grammar, or geology, which keep turning up. The tone of the speakers remains constantly neutral and even, even in the liveliest moments; the voices are polite, almost smiling despite the coolness and exactitude of their elocution. They all three know their parts down to the last comma, and the whole scenario is articulated like a piece of machinery, without a single hesitation, without a slip of memory or the tongue, in an absolute perfection.

The three actors are wearing dark suits of severe cut, with impeccable shirts and striped ties. They are sitting side by side on a little platform, behind a rickety wooden table, like the kind that used to be seen in poor men's kitchens. This piece of furniture is therefore more or less in harmony with the walls and ceiling of the room which are here, too, covered with the same dilapidated ceramic tiles, which slow infiltrations of moisture have loosened in irregular patches, revealing grayish surfaces of crude concrete, confined to the edges of the tile by crenellations or ladder-shaped areas. The theme of the day's lecture seems to be "the color red," considered as a radical solution to the irreducible antagonism between black and white.

Right now each of the three voices is devoted to one of the main liberating actions related to red: rape, arson, murder.

The preliminary section, which was ending when I arrived, must have been devoted to the theoretical justifications of crime in general and to the notion of metaphorical acts. The performers are now dealing with the identification and analysis of the three functions in particular. The reasoning which identifies rape with the color red, in cases where the victim has already lost her virginity, is of a purely subjective nature, though it appeals to recent studies of retinal impressions, as well as to investigations concerning the religious rituals of Central Africa, at the beginning of the century, and the lot of young captives belonging to races regarded as hostile, during public ceremonies suggesting the theatrical performances of antiquity, with their machinery, their brilliant costumes, their painted masks, their paroxysmal gestures, and that same mixture of coolness, precision, and delirium in the staging of a mythology as murderous as it is cathartic.

The crowd of spectators, facing the semicircle formed by the curved row of oil palms, dances from one foot to the other, stamping the red-earth floor, always in the same heavy rhythm which nonetheless gradually accelerates. Each time a foot touches the ground, the upper part of the body bends forward while the air emerging from the lungs produces a wheezing sound which seems to accompany some woodcutter's laborious efforts with his ax or some farmer's with his hoe. Without my being able to account for it, I keep remembering the sophisticated young woman disguised as a nurse who receives the so-called patients of Doctor Morgan in the brightly lighted little room precisely when she brushes past me with her dyed-blond hair and her doubtless artificial breasts that swell the white uniform and her violent perfume.

She prolongs the contact insistently, provocatively, inexplicably. As if an invisible obstacle stands in the middle of the room which she must pass on my side by undulating her hips in a kind of vertical slither, in order to get through the narrow space. And meanwhile, the stamping of bare feet on the clay floor continues in an accelerating cadence, accompanied by an increasingly raucous collective gasping, which finally drowns out the noise of the tom-toms beaten by musicians crouched in front of the dancing area, their row closing off the half-circle of palm trees.

But the three actors, on the dais, have now come to the second panel of their triptych, in other words, to the murder; and the demonstration can this time, on the contrary, remain on a perfectly objective level while being based on the blood spilled, provided nonetheless it is limited to methods provoking a sufficiently abundant external bleeding. The same is then the case for the third panel, which relates to the traditional color of flames, approached most nearly by using gasoline to start the fires.

The spectators, seated in parallel rows on their kitchen chairs, are as motionless in their religious attention as rag dolls. And since I have remained at the very back of the room, standing against the wall since there was no empty seat, and since as a result I see only their backs, I can suppose that they have no faces at all, that they are merely stuffed figures surmounted by clipped and curled wigs. The speakers, on their side, moreover, perform their parts in an altogether abstract fashion, always speaking quite frontally without their eyes coming to rest on anything, as if there were no one facing them, as if the room were empty.

And it is in chorus now, all three reciting the same text together, in the same neutral and jerky voices in which no syllable stands out, that they present the conclusion of the account: the perfect crime, which combines the three elements studied here, would be the defoliation, performed by force, of a virgin, preferably a girl with milky skin and very blond hair, the victim then being immolated by disembowelment or throat-cutting, her naked and bloodstained body having to be burned at a stake doused with gasoline, the fire gradually consuming the whole house.

The scream of terror, of pain, of death, still fills my ears as I contemplate the heap of crumpled bedclothes spread like so many rags on the floor, an improvised altar whose folds are gradually dyed a brilliant red, in a stain with distinct edges which, starting from the center, rapidly covers the entire area.

The fire on the contrary, once the match has grazed a shred of lace soaked in gasoline, spreads through the whole mass all at once, immediately doing away with the lacerated victim who is still stirring faintly, the heap of linen used in the sacrifice, the hunting knife, the whole room from which I have just had time to make my escape.

When I get to the middle of the corridor, I realize that the fire is already roaring in the elevator shaft, from top to bottom of the building, where I have lingered too long. Luckily there remained the fire escapes, zigzagging down the façade. Reversing my steps, then, I hurry toward the French window at the other end. It is locked. No matter how hard I press the catch in every direction, I cannot manage to release it. The bitter smoke fills my lungs and blinds me. With a sharp kick, aimed at the bottom of the window, I send the flat of my sole through four panes and their wooden frames. The broken glass tinkles shrilly as it falls out onto the iron platform. At the same time, reaching me along with the fresh air from outside and drowning out the roar of the flames, I hear the clamor of the crowd which has gathered in the street below.

I slip through the opening and I begin climbing down the iron steps. On all sides, at each floor, other panes are exploding because of the heat of the conflagration. Their tinkling sound, continuously amplified, accompanies me in my descent. I take the steps two at a time, three at a time.

Occasionally I stop a second to lean over the railing: it seems to me that the crowd at my feet is increasingly far away; I no longer even distinguish from each other the tiny heads raised toward me; soon there remains no more than a slightly blacker area in the gathering twilight, an area which is perhaps merely a reflection on the sidewalk gleaming after the recent shower. The shouts from a moment ago already constitute no more than a vague rustle which melts into the murmur of the city. And the warning siren of a distant fire engine, repeating its two plaintive notes, has something reassuring about it, something peaceful, something ordinary.

I close the French window, whose catch needs to be oiled. Now there is complete silence. Slowly I turn around to face Laura, who has remained a few feet behind me, in the passageway. "No," I say, "no one's there."

"All the same, he stayed out there, as if he was on sentry duty, all day long."

"Well, he's gone now."

In the corner of the recess formed by the building opposite, I have just caught sight of the black raincoat made even shinier by the rain glistening in the yellow light of a nearby streetlamp.

I ask Laura to describe to me the man she is talking about; she immediately gives me the information already known, in a slow voice, uncertain in its elocution but specific in its remembered details. I say, to make conversation: "Why do you think he is watching this particular house?"

"At regular intervals," she says, "he looks up toward the windows."

"Which windows?"

"This one and the ones of the two empty rooms on each side."

"Then he saw you at this one?"

"No, he couldn't have: I'm too far back and the room is too dark inside. The panes only reflect the sky."

"How do you know? Did you go out?"

"No! Oh no!" She seems panic-stricken at the idea. Then, a few seconds later, she adds, more calmly: "I figured it out—I made a sketch."

I say: "In any case, since he's gone, he must have been watching something else, or just waiting there, hoping that the rain would stop so he could be on his way."

"It didn't rain all day," she answers. And I can tell, from the sound of her voice, that in any case she doesn't believe me.

Once again I think that Frank must be right: this

girl represents a danger, because she tries to find out more than she can stand knowing. A decision will have to be made.

"Besides, he was already there yesterday," Laura says.

I take a step in her direction. She immediately steps back, keeping her timid eyes fixed on mine. I take another step, then a third. Each time, Laura retreats the same distance. "I'm going to have to . . ." I began, looking for the right words . . .

At that very moment, over our heads, we could hear something: low but distinctly audible, like three taps someone makes on a door if he wants to go into one of the rooms. All these rooms are empty, and there is no one but ourselves in the building. It might have been a beam creaking, which had seemed abnormally distinct to us because we ourselves were making so little noise, measuring our steps across the tiles. But Laura, half-whispering, said: "Did you hear that?"

"Hear what?"

"Someone knocking."

"No," I say, "that was me you heard."

I had then reached the stairs, and rested one hand on the banister. To reassure her, I tapped three times with the tip of one fingernail on the wooden rail without moving my palm or the other fingers. Laura gave a start and looked at my hand. I repeated my gesture, under her eyes. Despite the verisimilitude of my imitation, she must not have been altogether convinced. She has glanced up at the ceiling, then back at my hand. I have begun walking slowly toward her, and at the same time she has continued moving back.

She had almost reached the door of her room in

this manner, when once again we heard that same noise on the floor above. We both stopped and listened, trying to determine the place where it seemed to be coming from. Laura murmured in a very low voice that she was frightened.

I no longer had my hand on the railing, now, nor on anything at all. And it was difficult for me to invent something else of the same kind. "Well," I say, "I'll go up and see. But it's probably only a mouse."

I have turned around at once to return to the stairwell. Laura has hurried back into her room, trying to lock the door from inside with the key. In vain, of course, for the keyhole has been jammed ever since I put a nail into it, for just that purpose. As usual, Laura struggled a few moments, without managing to make the bolt work; then she gave up and walked over to the still open bed, where she has doubtless hidden herself, fully dressed. She has not even had to take off her shoes, since she is always barefoot, as I believe I have already indicated.

Instead of going up to the rooms above, I have immediately begun walking downstairs. The house, as I have said, consists of four identical stories, including the ground floor. There are five rooms on each floor, two of which look out on the street and two, in the rear, on the courtyard of a city school for girls; the last room, which faces the stairs, has no windows. At the level where we sleep, in other words the third floor, this blind room is a very large bathroom. We also use a few rooms of the ground floor: the one, for example, which I have called the library. All the rest of the house is uninhabited.

"Why?"

"The whole building includes, according to what I

have just said, twenty rooms. Which is far too many for two people."

"Why did you rent such a big house?"

"No, I'm not the tenant, only the watchman. The owners want to pull it down, so as to build something higher and more modern. If they were to rent apartments or rooms, that might create difficulties during the demolition."

"You haven't finished the story of the fire. What happened when the man coming down the fire escape reached the ground?"

"The firemen had put a little ladder between the lowest platform of the fire escape and the ground. The man with the gray face let himself tumble down, rather than actually climb the last rungs. The lieutenant fireman has asked him if there was still anyone in the building. The man has answered without a moment's hesitation that there was no one left. An elderly woman, who was in tears and had barely—as I understood it—escaped the flames, has repeated for the third time that a 'young lady,' who lived over her own room, had disappeared. The man has declared that the floor in question was empty, adding that doubtless this blond girl had already left her room when the fire broke out, perhaps in her very room: if she had forgotten to unplug an electric iron, or left on a gas burner, or an alcohol lamp . . ."

"And then what did you do?"

"I managed to lose myself in the crowd."

He finishes writing what interests him in the report I have just made. Then he looks up from his papers and asks, without my seeing the link with what has preceded: "Was the woman you call your sister in the house at that time?"

"Yes, of course, since she never goes out."

"You're sure of that?"

"Yes, absolutely sure."

Previously, and without any more reason, he had asked me how I accounted for the color of Laura's eyes, her skin, and her hair. I had answered that there had probably been some kind of mix-up. This interview over, I walked toward the subway, in order to go back home.

Meanwhile, Laura is still huddled under her sheets and blankets, pulled up over her mouth. But her eyes are wide open, and she is listening hard, trying to figure out what is happening overhead. Yet there is nothing to hear, so heavy and ominous is the silence of the whole house. At the end of the hallway, the murderer, who has quietly climbed up the fire escape, is now carefully picking up the pieces of broken glass which he found broken when he reached the window; thanks to the hole left by the little triangle of windowpane which had already fallen out, the man can grasp one by one between two fingers the sharp points which constitute the star and remove them by pulling them out from their groove between the wood frame and the dry putty. When he has, without hurrying, completed this task, he need merely thrust his hand through the gaping rectangle, where he no longer risks severing the veins in his wrist, and turn the recently oiled lock without making any noise at all. Then the window frame pivots silently on its hinges. Leaving it ajar, ready for his escape once his triple crime has been committed, the man in black gloves walks silently across the brick tiles.

Already the door handle moves slightly. The girl, half-sitting up in her bed, stares wide-eyed at the brass knob facing her. She sees the gleaming spot which is the reflection of the tiny bedlamp in the polished metal turning with unbearable deliberation. As if she were already feeling the sheets crushed beneath her covered with blood, she utters a scream of terror.

There is light under the door, since I have just pressed the hall-light button on my way up. I tell myself that Laura's screams will end by disturbing our neighbors. During the day, the schoolchildren hear them in their courtyard. I climb the stairs wearily, legs heavy, exhausted by a day of errands even more complicated than usual. I even need, tonight, the banister to lean on. At the second-floor landing, I carelessly drop my keys, which clatter against the iron bars before they reach the floor. I then notice that I have forgotten to set these keys down on the vestibule table downstairs, as I usually do each time I come in. I attribute this negligence to my exhaustion and to the fact that I was thinking about something else as I was closing my door: once again, about what Frank had just told me with regard to Laura, and which I should probably consider as an order.

This had happened at "Old Joe's." The band there makes such a racket that you can talk about your business without danger of being overheard by indiscreet ears. Sometimes the problem is actually to make yourself heard by the person you are talking to, whose face you get as close to as you can. At our table, there was also, at first, the go-between who calls himself Ben-Saïd, who as usual said nothing in the presence of the man whom we all more or less regard as the boss. But when Frank got up and walked toward the men's room (or, more likely, the telephone), Ben-Saïd told me right away that I was being followed and that he wanted to warn me. I pretended to be surprised and asked if he knew why.

"There are so many informers," he answered, "it's only natural to be careful." He added that in his opinion, moreover, almost all the active agents were watched.

"Then why tell me about it—me in particular?"

"Oh, just so you'll know."

I looked at the people at the other tables around us, and I said: "So my shadow is here tonight? You should tell me which one he is!"

"No," he answered without even turning his head to make sure, "here it's no use, there are almost no men here except our own. Besides, I think it's actually your house that's being watched."

"Why my house?"

"They think you're not living there alone."

"Yes I am," I say after a moment's thought, "I'm living alone there now."

"Maybe you are, but they don't seem to think so."

"They better let me know what they do think," I say calmly, to put an end to this conversation.

Frank was just coming back from the men's room. Passing by one of the tables, he said something to a man who immediately stood up and walked over to get his raincoat, hanging on a peg. Frank, who had continued on his way, then reached his chair. He sat down and said curtly to Ben-Saïd that everything was set, he should be on his way there now. Ben-Saïd left without asking for another word of information, even forgetting to say good-by to me. It was right after he left that Frank spoke to me about Laura. I listened without answering. When he finished: "That's it, you take it from there," I finished my Bloody Mary and went out.

In the street, just in front of the door, there were two homosexuals, walking arm in arm with their little dog on a leash. The taller one turned around and stared at me with an insistence I couldn't explain. Then he whispered something into his friend's ear, while they continued their stroll, walking with tiny steps. I thought that maybe I had a speck of dirt somewhere on my face. But when I rubbed the back of my hand over my cheeks, all I could feel were the hairs of my beard.

At the first shopwindow I came to, I stopped to examine my face in the glass. At the same time I took advantage of the occasion to glance back and I glimpsed Frank coming out of "Old Joe's." He was accompanied by Ben-Saïd, I am ready to swear to it, though the latter had already left at least three-quarters of an hour before. They were walking in the opposite direction from mine, but I was afraid one or the other would turn around, and I pressed up closer against the glass, as if the contents of the shopwindow were enormously interesting to me. It was only the wig-and-mask shop, though, whose display I have been familiar with for a long time.

The masks here are made out of some soft plastic material, very realistically fashioned, and bear no relation to those crude papier-mâché faces children wear at Halloween. The models are made to measure according to the customer's specifications. In the middle of the objects exhibited in the window, there is a large placard imitating hurriedly daubed-on graffiti: "If you don't like your hair, try ours. Feel like jumping out of your skin? Jump into ours!" They also sell foam-rubber gloves which completely replace the appearance of your hands—shape, color, etc.—by a new external aspect selected from a catalogue.

Framing the central slogan on all four sides, are neatly lined up the heads of some twenty presidents of the United States. One of them (I forget his name, but it's not Lincoln) is shown at the moment of his assassination, with the blood streaming down his face from a wound just over the brow ridge; but despite this detail, the facial expression is the calm smiling one which has been popularized by countless reproductions of every kind. These masks, even the ones without a bullet hole in them, must be on display only to indicate the extreme skill of the establishment (so that passers-by can discover the lifelike character of the resemblance to familiar features, including those of the president in office who is seen every day on the television screen); they are certainly not often used here in town, contrary to the anonymous faces which constitute the lower row, each accompanied by a brief caption to indicate its use and merits to the shop's clientele, for instance: "Psychoanalyst, about fifty, distinguished and intelligent; attentive expression despite the signs of fatigue which are the mark of study and hard work; worn preferably with glasses." And next to it: "Businessman, forty to forty-five, bold but serious; the shape of the nose indicates shrewdness as well as honesty; an attractive mouth, with or without mustache."

The wigs—for both sexes, but particularly for women—are set in the upper part of the window; in the middle, a long cascade of blond hair dangles in silky curls down to the forehead of one of the presidents. Finally, at the very bottom, paired on a strip of black velvet laid flat, false breasts (of all sizes, curves and hues, with various nipples and aureoles) are set out for—so it seems—at least two functions. As a matter of fact, a little diagram on one side shows the way of attaching them to the chest (with a variant for male bodies), as well as the way of keeping the edges imperceptible, for only this delicate point can betray the device, so perfect is the imitation of the flesh as well as of the texture of the skin. And elsewhere, however, one of these objects—which also belongs to a pair, the second breast being intact—has been riddled with many needles of various sizes, to show that it can also be used as a pincushion. All the facsimiles exhibited here are so lifelike that it is surprising not to see forming, on the pearly surface of this last one, tiny ruby drops.

The hands are scattered all over the shopwindow. Some are arranged so as to form anecdotal elements in contact with some other article: a woman's hand on the mouth of the old "avant-garde artist," two hands parting a mass of auburn hair, a very black hand—a man's hand—squeezing a pale pink breast, two powerful hands clutching the neck of the "movie starlet." But most of the hands soar through the air, agile and diaphanous. It even seems to me that there are a lot more of them tonight than on other days. They move gracefully, hanging on invisible threads; they open their fingers, turn over, revolve, close. They really look like the hands of lovely women recently severed —several of them, moreover, have blood still dripping from the wrist, chopped off on the block with one stroke of a well-sharpened axe.

And the decapitated heads too—I had not noticed it

at first—are bleeding profusely, those of the assassinated presidents, but all the rest even more: the lawyer's head, the psychoanalyst's, the car salesman's, Johnson's, the waitress's, Ben-Saïd's, the trumpet-player at "Old Joe's" this week, and the head of the sophisticated nurse who receives patients for Doctor Morgan in the corridors of the subway station of the line I then take to get back home.

On my way upstairs, as I reach the second-floor landing, I happen to drop my keys, which ring against the iron bars of the banister before falling on the last step. It is then that Laura, at the end of the corridor, begins screaming. Luckily, her door is never locked. I walk into her room, where I find her half-naked, crouching in terror on her rumpled bed. I calm her by the usual methods.

Then she asks me to tell her about my day. I tell her about the example of arson which has destroyed a whole building on One Hundred and Twenty-third Street. But since she soon starts asking too many questions, I change the subject by telling her the story—I saw it myself only a little while later—of that ordinary couple who visited the mask-maker on the advice of the family physician: they each wanted to order the other's face, in order to be able to act out in reverse the psychodrama of their conjugal difficulties. Laura seems amused by this situation, to such a degree in fact that she forgets to ask me what I was doing in such a shop and how I could have managed to hear what was said. I do not tell her that the shopkeeper works with us, nor that I suspect him of being a cop. Nor do I tell her about JR's disappearance and the investigations into her case which have taken up most of my working time.

It is at the office that I hear the news. I have already told how this office works. To all appearances, it is a placement office of the United Manichean Church. But in reality, the domestics by-the-month, lady's companions or various slaves, the part-time secretaries, the high-school-student baby-sitters, the call girls paid by the hour, etc., are so many information agents—of organized crime and propaganda—which we thereby manage to introduce into the establishment. The rings of call girls, high-class prostitutes and concubines obviously constitute our best cases, since from them we get both irreplaceable contacts with men in office and also the larger part of our financial resources, not to mention the possibility of blackmail.

JR had been placed as a baby-sitter the week before, in answer to a tiny advertisement in *The New York Times*: "Unmarried father wants young girl, pleasant appearance, docile character, for night sessions with rebellious child." The child in question actually existed, despite the oddly promising text of the advertisement: the words "docile" and "authoritarian" figuring, as is well known, high on the list of specialists' code words. In principle, what was involved should have been the participation in the training of a novice mistress, giving her if need be a good example of submission.

Therefore we sent JR, a handsome white girl with a fine head of auburn hair which always creates a good effect in intimate scenes, who had already handled similar cases on several occasions. She arrives that same evening at the address given, on Park Avenue, between Fifty-sixth and Fifty-seventh Streets, wearing a very short, close-fitting green silk dress which has always given us good results. To her great surprise, it is a little girl of twelve or a little older who opens the door; she is alone in the apartment, she says in answer to JR's embarrassed question, her name is Laura, she is thirteen and a half, and she offers JR a glass of bitter lemon while they chat, to get to know each other . . .

JR insists: "I really wanted to see your father . . ." But the little girl immediately declares, quite offhandedly, that in the first place that is impossible, since he's gone out, and besides, "you know, he's not really my father . . . ," these last words whispered in a much lower tone, confidentially, with a tiny smothered laugh to end the sentence in a very good imitation of polite embarrassment. Having absolutely no interest in the problem of adopted or illegitimate children, JR would have been ready to leave right away, if the opulence of the house—the avant-garde millionaire style—hadn't made her stay after all, to satisfy her professional conscience. So she drank the lemon the little girl served her in a kind of boudoir where the seats and little tables were inflated by pressing on electric buttons. To make conversation, and also because it might be a useful piece of information under other circumstances, she asked if there were no servants.

"Well, there's you," Laura answered, with her prettiest smile.

"No, I mean, to do the housework, the cooking . . ."

"You don't plan to do any housework?"

"Well, I . . . I didn't think that was what I came for . . . There's no one else?"

The little girl's expression now contrasted with her previous simperings of a child pretending to be the lady of the house. And in a very different tone of voice, remote and as though filled with melancholy, or despair, she finally said, as if with great reluctance: "There's a black woman, mornings."

Then neither of us said another word for what seemed to me quite a long time. Laura sipped her bitter lemon. I decided she was unhappy, but I wasn't there to deal with that question. And at that moment, there were steps in the next room, heavy and determined steps on a creaking floorboard; at first I didn't think of how old it was to have that kind of floor in such an apartment building. I said: "Is there someone next door?"

The child answered: "No," with that same remote expression.

"But I just heard someone walking . . . Listen, there it is again! . . ."

"No, it can't be, there's never anyone there," she answered, in her most stubborn manner, against all appearances.

"Then perhaps you have neighbors?"

"No, there are no neighbors. This is all the apartment!" And with a sweeping gesture, she included the vicinity of the boudoir in all directions.

Nonetheless she got up from her pneumatic chair and took a few nervous steps to the large bay window which seemed to open onto nothing but the unvarying gray sky. That was when I noticed how silent her own footsteps remained on the white carpeting thick as fleece, even when she tapped on the floor with her little black patent-leather shoes.

If little Laura's intention had been to drown out by her movements the noises of the adjoining room, it was a miscalculation in any case, especially since they continued all the louder behind the partition, from which came now the quite recognizable echoes of a struggle: trampling, furniture knocked over, heavy breathing, clothes ripped, and even, soon after, groans, muffled pleas, as though uttered by a woman who for unknown reasons dares not raise her voice, or is materially prevented from doing so.

The little girl, too, was listening now. When the moaning assumed a more particular character, she gave me a sidelong glance, and I had the impression that a fugitive smile passed across her lips, or at least between her half-closed eyelids which had perceptibly winked. But then there was a fierce scream, so violent that she made up her mind to go and see, though without seeming in any way surprised or alarmed.

Having left my seat at the same moment, in an instinctive movement, I saw the door close behind Laura; then, since there was nothing more to be heard, I turned my head toward the sheet of glass. I was thinking, of course, of the fire escape; but aside from the fact that no such thing exists on any building of recent construction, I would have been very reluctant to use, once again, this convenient means of regaining the street, the subway, my abandoned house . . . In a few meditative steps, however, I reach the huge bay window, and raise the thick tulle curtains covering it.

I am then amazed to discover that the room we were in overlooks Central Park, which seems to me quite impossible, given the position of the building JR entered a few minutes earlier. It would have required, in other words, that the complicated route she took to the apartment door from the entrance lobby, by various elevators and escalators, made her pass under at least one street. But now these topographical reflections divert me to a scene which is taking place at the very bottom, between the bushes, not far from a streetlamp casting a dim light over the figures, distorting their shadows.

There are three men, or else two men and a woman, it is difficult to tell exactly, seen from so high up and in such a dim light. It is equally impossible to say with any certainty if the white car parked nearby, at the curb, is involved with the wild gesticulations, the rapid, repeated, apparently incoherent comings and goings of the three individuals. What is certain, on the other hand, is that they are carrying out some hasty and secret operation: tearing up flowers, or else carrying and concealing under the vegetation objects of rather small size, or perhaps even changing clothes with each other, or rather putting on clothes brought intentionally, after having thrown into the bushes, bordering the flower bed, the ones they had previously been wearing and which they now wanted to get rid of . . . It is even conceivable that they are completing their transformations by taking off the masks they had been wearing for the criminal act they have just committed, also removing like gloves the white hands with false fingerprints which camouflaged their black skin.

One of the men, who is not managing to get rid of his mask, too well pasted onto his real face, hurrying to finish, for the morals squad looking for under-age homosexuals is always a danger in these neighborhoods, loses patience, strips off at random the various lumps or protrusions on which he can get a grip, and begins tearing at his ears, his throat, his temples, his eyelids, without even realizing that he is actually lacerating in his haste big sections of his own flesh.

And in a little while, when he appears in "Old Joe's" to report to Frank on his mission and to recoup his strength with a double shot of bourbon, the band will suddenly stop playing, the trumpet-player suddenly mute, without thinking in his astonishment of putting down his meaningless instrument, will merely take it away from his mouth, holding it motionless in the air about three inches from his lips which still keep the tense position of a soloist in the middle of a fortissimo, while all the heads in the room turn with a single movement toward the street door, in order to see in their turn what the musicians have seen first from the bandstand: the bloody face which has just appeared in the rectangular frame formed by the open door against the black background of the night.

As for me, I believe I have now looked long enough at the window where the rows of masks of the dead presidents surround the placard which permits any plan, any fantasy, and I risk another sidelong glance toward the end of the street, where I think I once again see the figures of Frank and Ben-Saïd walking away. But this glance may be too brief to permit me to register anything but the series of houses whose irregular façades succeed each other down the empty street, which I then project for a long time through the shop-window quickly returned to like a refuge, inside which glows the luxuriant auburn hair which offers its abundance just opposite my gaze.

Finally I make up my mind to look more openly in the other direction: contrary to my calculations, the two men have actually vanished. Not having had time, without running, to reach the intersection, they can only have gone into a building next door to "Old

Joe's." So all I have to do now is to head toward the subway station and then return home.

But in the express car, quite empty as it often is at this late hour, which is carrying me in a tremendous racket of grating machinery, vibrating metal, and irregular jolts, I think again of JR who is still, meanwhile, with little Laura in the Park Avenue apartment. The child has finally made up her mind to show her new governess where the disturbing sounds come from that filled the room next door: a tape inside a transparent plastic cassette, set on a Chinese stand. The scene of violence has calmed down now; all that can be heard is an irregular, still-oppressed breathing which gradually fades into the silence of the great building.

JR asks the little girl why she puts such strange recordings into this machine. But Laura continues listening without a word to the breathing box, her eyes fixed on the slender brown tape which smoothly unrolls behind its transparent plate, from which the young woman cannot even manage to tear her eyes, in the imperceptibly anxious expectation of what will happen next.

Then the child makes up her mind to answer, but without taking her eyes off the cassette in which one of the reels gradually loses its thickness while the other's diameter increases. The tone of her voice is that of a discreet, neutral commentary, which seems to be the result of her attentive observation of the mechanism: "He turned it on before he went out," she says.

"But you could have turned it off!"

"No, you can't turn it off: the box is locked."

"Did your father forget to turn it off before he went out?"

"He's not my father, and he didn't forget: he started it on purpose."

"Why?"

"He said it's to keep me company."

"When I came in, you couldn't hear a thing."

"Because you came in during a silence."

"Are there silences on the tape?"

"Yes . . . Sometimes very long ones . . ." And she adds in a low voice, keeping her face bent over the little machine: "Those are the times I'm really frightened . . ."

"But . . . Couldn't you tell him . . ."

"No, it's no use . . . He does it on purpose."

And suddenly the action resumes, without warning, with a man's footsteps, once again, hurrying footsteps climbing up steps, metallic echoes coming closer from landing to landing, faster and faster, nearer and nearer, until they give the impression that someone is right here in the room, and at this moment a loud noise of broken glass makes us both give a start and turn our heads in the same movement toward the bay window . . . But it is only the tape which continues its slow and continuous unwinding . . . Pieces of glass have fallen tinkling to the tiles; then come the fainter noises of the pieces of glass carefully being removed, then a latch grating, a window opening, the footsteps advancing down the tiled corridor, a very long corridor, a door brutally opened, a young woman's scream quickly smothered in the sound of cloth being torn, and a hoarse voice murmuring: "Keep still, you little fool, or I'll hurt you . . ."

Then Laura gently raises the light lid of the transparent box, presses a precise finger on a tiny red button, and everything stops.

"That's enough for now," she says, "it's always the same: the footsteps, the screams, the broken glass, and they keep saying the same thing."

"Where does it come from?"

"What—the cassette?"

"No, the tape."

"From the man who sells them—where do you think it would come from?"

"But . . . Who recorded it?"

"The musicians, of course, the performers!"

"And they sell it in the stores?"

"Of course! I bought this one this morning, in the Times Square subway station . . . It's the story of a lieutenant fireman who climbs up a skyscraper to save a little girl who's about to throw herself off."

"Oh, I see . . . She wants to kill herself?"

"Yes."

"Why?"

"Because she doesn't have enough fun at home."

"And why did she say that her father started the tape and locked the cassette?"

"First of all she didn't say he was her father. And besides, she never stops lying anyway."

"Does she like lying?"

"Not all that much. But for one little truth, there are millions and millions of lies, so she can't help it, really . . . And she might have said, just as well, that it was the lieutenant fireman who made her listen to this on purpose to scare her; or that it was you, or me, or Abraham Lincoln, or Edouard Manneret."

JR glances at her watch. It is almost midnight. She's tired of waiting. She asks: "And what time is your stepfather coming back?"

"My stepfather? Oh yes, my uncle, you mean . . .

He's not coming back today. If you want to leave, you can. There's a time clock in the vestibule—if you punch it, you'll be paid automatically: I punched it for you when you rang, at the same time I turned on the cassette."

Young Laura immediately accompanies her visitor to the apartment door, which she slams behind her, shouting "See you soon!" words followed by the sharp click of the lock, which extends a deep vibration through the entire wooden panel.

Then an angelic smile curves the little girl's lips, as she listens to the echo which rises, fades, and quickly dies away . . . Then she returns, dancing in a slow waltz, steps to the Chinese room, reopens the plexiglass cassette, turns back the reels without bothering to bring them all the way to the starting position, presses the red button and stretches out on the floor to listen to the other side in peace:

". . . did auburn hair which offers its splendor just opposite me. It immediately occurs to me that this is a trap: the too knowingly sensual and accessory smile of this young woman from nowhere, on the strength of a simple advertisement, and who has told me nothing about herself so far except her first name: Joan, her dress too short and cut too low, its fine emerald-green silk shifting too readily over a tender, firm flesh, gentle, nervous, and as though too provisionally concealed by those green algae with their shifting reflections, vague, impalpable areas changing slowly, according to secret currents, drowned in the liquid mass a deep-sea fish whose motionless body, half-hidden in the ulvae, faintly undulates itself occasionally, ready to buckle in sudden violent twists, ready to open in a soft and greedy mouth with complicated, precise, many-formed folds, ceaselessly reshaped by new excrescences or invaginations, but which despite their shifting sinuosities preserve a constant bilateral symmetry."

"Oh, come on . . ." Laura says aloud, to express her lack of enthusiasm for this last detail, emphasizing her condemnation by a critical pout of her pursed lips. Then she suddenly stands up, in an unlikely leap, and seizes an enormous dictionary which seems to be, on most occasions, within arm's reach. She looks up the word "ulva" and reads: "a genus of green seaweeds, the sea-lettuces, with a thin, flat thallus like a lettuce leaf, generally growing in brackish waters." The little girl stares at the carved cornice which runs under the ceiling, at the top of the scarlet-wallpapered room, thinking that a deep-sea fish cannot take refuge in that salad. Then she whispers, though quite distinctly: "ulva oluptuous," and a few seconds later, "submerged cathedral."

She walks over to the bay window, in order to see if the thieves hidden in the bushes lining the avenue have found any victims. But nothing more is to be seen in the narrow zone illuminated by the streetlamp; perhaps they have caught their prey and are now dismembering it, under cover of the foliage. Their victim is probably the pretty governess, who was caught as she came out of the building.

Laura lets the tulle curtain fall back, glances at the cassette and notices that the reel is far from being finished; and the voice, which has meanwhile continued telling its story, seems to have been scarcely disturbed by something more interesting: uproar of a revolution, sirens, conflagration, revolver shots. . . . Then the little girl herself imitates a burst of machine-gun fire, staggers and collapses in a heap on the high-pile carpet, where she remains lying on her back at full length, legs and arms spread out in a cross.

This tape is certainly not worth much, on either side. The narrator continues his reasons to suspect a pretty girl named Joan, the latest of the governesses recruited by means of an advertisement in the newspaper. He has the impression of having got hold, this time, of what he is looking for, but he must not make any mistake: even if the auburn-haired young woman is really a prostitute—amateur or professional—it still remains to be proved that she belongs to the organization; and to be sure of that, he must be careful not to force matters. The conversation with Laura, during her first visit—duly recorded by the microphones hidden in the walls—actually warranted only the vaguest suppositions. The second meeting, with the uncle himself, as just reported, has therefore already supplied more tangible results. The third time, JR is asked to come in the middle of the afternoon.

She arrives as arranged, at the Park Avenue address, and rings as usual at the door of the sham apartment. The door turns slowly on its hinges, without anyone, today, appearing in the vestibule. And it is the time clock which announces cavernously: "Come in . . . Close the door . . . Thank you . . . Your arrival has been recorded."

Since the vestibule remains empty, JR walks into the pneumatic boudoir, where she finds no one either. But she hears a man's voice—which she thinks she recognizes—in the next room, the Chinese one. She knocks lightly on the door, receives no answer, decides to walk into the sanctuary all the same, wearing her best smile—the smile of a timid slave secretly in love with her master (since the word "docile" has not yet been clarified) . . . But the smile freezes on her lovely lips: little Laura is here, lying full length on the floor, and it is the tape recorder that is talking.

JR reaches the lacquered table in a few nervous steps; she lifts up the lid of the transparent box and stops the machine with an irritated gesture. The child has not stirred.

JR asks: "Isn't your uncle here?"

Without making a move, Laura answers: "No, as you see."

JR insists: "He's not at home:"

"If he was at home, you wouldn't have to come and take care of me."

"Fine . . . I'd like to know what need there is to take care of a girl your age as if she was a baby."

"If you hadn't come, I would have set fire to the apartment. I had already prepared the can of gasoline and the pile of sheets."

The young woman shrugs her shoulders and says: "Don't you go to school?"

"No."

"Ever?"

"No. Why should I?"

"Oh, to learn something."

"What?"

"What a job!" JR thinks, as she walks back and forth in the room. She approaches the large bay window, raises the curtain, returns to the prone body which now rolls across the red carpet as if it were suffering from epileptic convulsions. She feels like giving it a good kick.

"Oh, I don't know," she says, "variable equations, or the capital of Maryland . . ."

"Annapolis!" the little girl shrieks. "That's too easy. Ask another question."

"Who killed Lincoln?"

"John Wilkes Booth."

"How many seconds are there in a day?"

"Eighty-six thousand four hundred and twenty."

"What's an ulva?"

"A genus of green seaweeds."

"What do little girls dream about?"

"Knives . . . and blood!"

"Where are the women we love?"

"In the grave."

"How old are you?"

"Thirteen and a half."

"What do you see from the windows of this apartment?"

"Central Park."

(That's what it had looked like to me.)

"Is this part of it lit?"

"Yes, dimly . . . There's a streetlamp."

"And what can be seen near the streetlamp?"

"Three people."

"Of which sex?"

"Two men, a woman . . . She's wearing pants and a cap, but you can see her breasts under her sweater."

"What is this lady's name?"

"Her name—or at least what they call her—is Joan Robeson, or sometimes Robertson too."

"What does she do?"

"She's one of the fake nurses who works for Doctor Morgan, the psychoanalyst whose office is in the Forty-second Street subway station. The other nurses are blond, and . . ."

"But what is she doing here, now, in the bushes

bordering the park, with those two men? And who are those two men?"

"That's easy: one is Ben-Saïd, the other is the narrator. The three of them are loading cartons of marijuana cigarettes disguised as ordinary Philip Morrises into a white Buick. It was a go-between who dropped them in the bushes a few minutes ago; he had just heard, by a walkie-talkie radio, that his car was going to be searched by the police when it reached the garage. Who could have warned him? A cop, of course, who was working with them. Joan and the other two have been assigned to make the pickup. What makes it hard to understand their gestures is that they are not content to lean down, to grope for the packages scattered in the foliage, hiding them one after the other under their clothes and carrying them that way to the car parked at the curb; for the same time they are eating roast-beef sandwiches which they have to keep stuffing into their pockets in order not to interrupt their work, pulling them out again the next minute.

Ben-Saïd hasn't opened his mouth since the job began, except to bite into his sandwich, and the narrator wonders if something's wrong, for he's usually quite talkative. Joan, who has concealed her hair, for the occasion, under a huge cap, smiles or winks at him playfully, each time she comes near him; without much effect, moreover, for he seems to pay no attention to her. Irritated by their behavior, the narrator —let's say "I," it will be simpler—looks around for a long time to make sure nothing is left behind the clump of japonica; and this is the moment the girl chooses to come over and search in the same place, as if she hadn't seen that someone was already there.

"Oh, there you are!" she says.

"Yes, you can see I am . . . What's the matter with Ben-Saïd?"

"Nothing . . . problems . . ."

"But what?"

"Apparently you've been making an ass of yourself, and he's going to be turned in . . . because of you."

"Oh? . . . Why him?"

"Because Frank gave him orders to take care of you, and he doesn't want to play informer."

"He's a good guy! . . . What kind of an ass?"

"You've been hiding someone at your place, someone who was supposed to be taken care of a long time ago."

"Oh, so that's it."

"I told him he was crazy."

"Thanks a lot. And what do you really think?"

She does not answer immediately. She pretends to think she's going to find another carton by picking up three dead leaves. Then she straightens up and stares right at me, as though by accident, with a kind of calculated insistence. I have already said, I think, that her lips are fleshy, sharp-edged, shiny as if they were always faintly moist; and her face is like warm milk, in the darkness. I'd like someone to tell me, some day, how much Puerto Rican blood this pretty whore is supposed to have.

"Well," she says, too slowly, "I think he's crazy, of course."

When she talks, her mouth moves in the half-darkness of the depths: like some aquatic animal whose wavering curves constantly shift, but without ever losing their lovely symmetry, suggesting those ink blots you spread on a sheet of paper folded in half.

58

"All right, fine," I say, "and it would be better for you to mind your own business." But I immediately regret this useless remark. As a matter of fact, I thought I made out a gleam of hatred and violence in her big green eyes. Naturally it can only be my imagination: it is not even light enough, here in the bushes, to make out the color of her eyes, if I didn't know it already.

JR straightens up calmly, with the gesture of a wild animal, with twists and curves that seem to be filmed in slow motion. Without hurrying, she begins moving away. The naked flesh of her round white neck gleams like a knife blade when she passes under the direct light of the streetlamp.

I say, trying to seem better-humored: "And the man with the want ad—how's that going?"

"Fine," she answers, "thanks."

"Are you going back there?"

"Yes, tonight. But it would be better for you to mind your own business."

Watching her head casually for the car, I was thinking that she must have as beautiful a body as they say, to show it off that way in stretch pants and a sweater. It occurs to me, at the same time, what a lovely corpse you could make out of that lovely white flesh.

Straightening up, I felt a sharp pain in my knees, stiff from the position my legs had been in for too long. While the joints recovered their normal function, I rubbed my hands together two or three times, to brush off the little pieces of dirt or dry twigs that had stuck against the palms and finger tips.

It was that night that we lost all contact with her. I heard about her disappearance the next day, when I reached the office, without having seen her again myself since the business with the cigarettes. We had not said anything else before we separated; the load was all there: there was the same number of packages as on the shipping list. JR drove the Buick back to the garage herself, the night man confirmed her arrival there at the usual time. She left right away in her own car, in order to go home and change: she took a bath, washed her hair, perfumed her entire body and made up carefully; then she decided to press the green silk dress she was supposed to wear that night, as has already been said. The only jewelry she wore was a tiny gold chain she slipped over her head, with a simple cross attached to it.

"And what did Ben-Saïd do after he left her?"

"I don't recall that he was particularly concerned about her. I myself was busy with the counting and checking of the cigarette cartons. When the Buick drove away, Ben-Saïd grumbled some vague good night, and I think I remember that he made some ironic allusion, between his teeth, to the rumors of a big fire we could hear in the distance, toward Harlem. Then he vanished between the trees, doubtless intending to walk across the park toward Columbia. I took the subway, as usual, to get home. There I found Laura, who was very upset because I was late. I briefly explained the reason for the delay, but in order not to risk making her even more nervous by reawakening her own memories, I didn't mention JR's disappearance; I have already described this deliberate omission, as well as all the rest of my evening."

"All right . . . The garage you're talking about is in lower Manhattan, at the entrance to the tunnel; JR's apartment is the one on a Hundred and Twenty-third Street?"

"Yes, that's right."

"How much time do you think she can have taken to get from Central Park to the tunnel, and then to drive back up as far as Harlem?"

"It was late, the streets were empty . . ."

"How do you know, since you went home by subway?"

"I took the subway at the Madison Avenue station."

"That's not very convenient, if you were going home."

"It's not much longer. And it's easier to change."

"Where did you get those details, about her bath, her perfume, the green dress, since you say you didn't see her again?"

"It's the outfit she was supposed to wear on such occasions. It's all written on her punch card, in the office files."

"Even the little gold cross?"

"Yes, of course."

"But how can you know about her deciding to press her dress?"

"She told us about it when she left: 'I have to get going so I can press my dress!' "

"Yet you have just indicated, in your report, that you hadn't exchanged any further conversation with her, after the little argument in the japonicas. Perhaps she was telling Ben-Saïd that business about her dress?"

"Yes, probably."

"Then Ben-Saïd could confirm her intention to press her dress?"

"No, I don't think so—he didn't hear her. I've already said that he wasn't paying attention right then.

Besides, it must have been a little earlier that she said that, before our discussion . . . You called it an argument just now; no, that's an exaggeration: they were just ordinary words, nothing special, things we said while we were doing our work."

"One last question: you say you didn't indicate, that night, to the woman you call your sister, that JR had disappeared. How could you have done so, since you didn't know she had disappeared? And since there could have been no question of anything of that kind, as a matter of fact?"

"You're right, I hadn't thought of that. So it would be only the next morning that I must have thought of hiding that disappearance from her."

"If your suppositions are confirmed, Joan—at that hour—is still at home, calmly pressing her dress and glancing absently at the night program on the television screen. Since the apartment is overheated, she has not bothered, as she leaves the bathroom, to put on a robe or any other garment. Only her high-heeled green leather shoes and her black stockings, embellished with a narrow ruffle of pink lace instead of a garter at the top of her thighs. Above this line, all she lacks is her dress, which she will put on as soon as she completes the task over which she is bending so industriously now; in other words, all that she is wearing, besides, at this moment, is her little gold cross.

On the white sheet covering the little tapering ironing-board, she has also laid a pair of large chromium-steel sewing scissors which she has just used to cut a thread hanging from the seam of the lower hem; the two sharp blades, open in a V, gleam in the light of a gooseneck lamp whose light they reflect in a crisscross of rays. Not far away, at the same height as the board, the curly hair of her pubic area (of modest dimensions and perfectly equilateral triangular shape) is of the same shining bright red as the long hair which, after the movement of the iron, resumes its natural position over the curve of her shoulders, until it is raised in a loose bun, ready to tumble down at the lightest touch.

Occasionally, the young woman glances at the little screen, which shows a documentary film about the religious ceremonies of central Africa, in the course of which seven young girls of noble rank, belonging to vanquished tribes, are to be impaled on the sexual organ of the fertility god, in the sacred shade of the oil palms laden with their fruit and—the narrator adds—to the obsessive rhythm of the war drums. It does not seem, according to the uniform hue of the protagonists, that the conflicts which are at the source of these customs can be imputed to the unreconcilable coloring of their skin; the only notable difference, as a matter of fact, is that the skin of the captives remains entirely visible, since they are naked, while that of the executioners and the musicians partly disappears under masks and crude geometric patterns daubed with white paint. In any case, the color television set is very effective for this kind of film, which is called, moreover, *The Red and the Black*. JR stops a moment in her work, the iron suspended in mid-air about eight inches from the green silk, staring at the executions shown in closeup. The tip of her tongue still sticks out between her lips, as it always does when she performs some exacting domestic task, according to a childhood habit.

At the most interesting moment, a tiny smile of satisfaction passes like the shadow of a bird of prey over her porcelain face, while the pink tongue slowly returns to its place. And while the blood gushes down the inner surface of the brown thighs which are gradually covered by a scarlet network, the young woman unconsciously begins caressing herself against the pointed end of the felt-covered ironing-board. This is the moment when she heard the balcony window opening behind her.

The moment has come, then, to describe exactly how things are arranged. This apartment is one with modern equipment and decoration, in a building about fifty years old. Inside it is all polished surfaces, whiteness, mirrors, reflections, sharp corners, whereas against the brick façade of the building rises the zigzag frame of the black iron fire escape . . .

But these metal steps have already been used too often—as has been observed several times over—and the killer, arriving ahead of JR, has chosen to get into the apartment by using a skeleton key (there are always a number at the office, for all the locks of our various agents), and then, without difficulty, to climb out on the balcony, pulling the window shut after him in such a way as to suggest that it is closed as usual, and to wait there for the right moment. The girl, in effect, has had no suspicions. She undressed immediately. But he has preferred to give her time to wash and perfume her body. Then, he had no need for a freshly ironed dress, it was only the television documentary—which he too was watching from behind the pane—which somewhat delayed his appearance. Nor was this time wasted, moreover, for it allowed him to notice, according to the sounds which reached him from the other windows, that the neighbors were all tuned in to the same program, the only possible one, no doubt, at this late hour. The continuous pounding of the war drums and the endless shouting on the sound track will therefore greatly facilitate his enterprise, giving him plenty of time to stage the murder according to his tastes.

But now a preliminary question arises: how could JR have heard the window opening, when it was not even really closed, during such a racket? Unless such a detail is utterly without consequence (since it would change nothing in the episode if the murderer had come up to his victim from behind, without her realizing he was there), it might very well be the sudden cold on her naked flesh which has made her turn around.

Whatever the case she then sees a uniformed policeman (it is a fake uniform and a mask that the man is wearing, but she can hardly be aware of the fact) who, regulation pistol aimed at her belly, advances toward her, ordering her to keep still and not to move. Raising her hands in the air in astonishment, though she has not been asked to do so, she drops the hot iron on her green dress, where, the thermostat being jarred in its fall, it will leave a large triangular hole in the pubic area. As for the iron fire escape—now that I think of it—it will be used after all: to make a getaway while the fire breaks out, as has already been described.

At the bottom of the ladder which connects the last landing and the sidewalk, the firemen, who are still looking for possible arsonists, seem immediately reassured by the black raincoat, the boots, the leather shoulder strap, the officer's stripes and the visored cap (the gun has remained upstairs).

"You're a brave man," the chief says in a tough voice. "You didn't see anything abnormal?"

"No, captain, everything's all right. No one is left in the house. You can go ahead."

"A case of arson?"

"No—an iron with a defective thermostat."

A few minutes later, the whole building collapses in the uproar of an explosion. (In New York, when a building is on fire and the firemen have no hope of extinguishing the blaze by means of their hoses before the flames reach the adjacent structures, it is a practice to destroy the damaged building at once by means of dynamite, whose explosion does more work in one second than a thousand tons of water, according to a procedure worked out for oil wells.) Afterward, all I had to do was to take the subway in order to get home.

Ben-Saïd, who has also been listening, in silence, to the sirens and the final explosion, broke his silence momentarily to murmur something about "the monstrous negligence of the authorities." Since he never smiles, I cannot swear this was a joke. Then he left, walking alone across the park. He vanished almost immediately into the darkness. When I reached home myself . . .

"Could your young sister testify to exactly what time it was when you got there?"

"No, certainly not—she never has a clock in sight, nor a watch on her wrist, nor anything that might allow her to give that kind of information. You know there's no telephone in the building any more: it's been turned off because of the imminent demolition; so Laura can't even call to find out the time from the operator. This total ignorance of time in which she has been kept is the consequence of a decision taken with the doctor's advice: any reference to time—as I have already said—awakens her anxiety. The disadvantage of the present system is that now she always imagines that I am late; and if my work at the office or elsewhere has actually lasted longer than usual, she has the impression of a much greater delay than is actually the case. This evening, for example, I find her waiting for me at the library door, on the ground floor, holding an open book as if she had just interrupted her reading when she heard my key turning in the lock of the door to the building; I know perfectly well that as a matter of fact she has been standing there, in that position, for at least an hour, listening for the sounds of my return. She is standing in the . . ."

"What kind of book was she holding?"

"A detective story, of course: that's all there is in the house, and very few of those, so that she is always reading the same ones over and over. The walls of this large ground-floor room are covered with shelves, from floor to ceiling; but they are all empty, or almost all; we still call it the library, because of its initial purpose. Without having to turn around, I immediately notice, in the mirror over the vestibule table, on the marble top of which I set down my keys when I come in each evening, that the book pressed against Laura's dress, at the height of the pubic region, held open by the forefinger marking her place, does not belong to our scant collection. The cover, whose colors are at once loud and dull according to the tradition of the genre, nonetheless remind me of none of the ones familiar to me, which I even know by heart down to their last detail, having encountered them almost everywhere in the house, set down at random on the furniture, cluttering up the tables and chairs, lying on the floor, which has always suggested to me that Laura was reading all these books at once and that in this way she mixed up from room to room, according to her own movements, the itineraries of the detectives carefully calculated by the author, thereby endlessly altering the arrangement of each volume, leaping moreover a hundred times a day from one work to the next, not minding her frequent returns to the same passage nonetheless stripped of any apparent interest, whereas she utterly abandons on the contrary the essential chapter which contains the climax of an investigation, and consequently gives its whole meaning to the rest of the plot; and all the more since many of these mass-produced bindings having failed to withstand the occasionally brutal negligence of this way of reading, they have lost, over the months, a corner of a page, here and there a whole page, or even two or three signatures all at once.

But, if a new volume (not new, for this one seems in a condition resembling that of the others) has just been introduced into the cycle, it must be that someone has come here in my absence. Laura herself cannot go out, since, for safety's sake, I lock the door when I leave. Someone from outside, on the other hand, might perfectly well be in possession of a skeleton key or a burglar's kit, or might even have a key made for himself by a locksmith, saying it is the key to his house and that he has lost his own, tonight, during a struggle with three hoodlums in an empty subway car.

Under the astonished eyes of the man in the felt hat pulled down over his eyes, still at his post in the recess of the house across the street only a little closer to the

corner in order to observe the unexpected scene without danger of being noticed, while he once again, with
a mechanical gesture, stuffs his black-gloved hands
into the deep pockets of his raincoat glistening with
rain, the locksmith arrives, then, and tranquilly goes
about his work at the top of the outside steps, with all
his equipment, which he sets down on the doorstep
after having checked, in a little notebook with a worn
cover, removed a moment before from his jacket, that
the number of the building corresponds with the one
given by his customer, who has not been able to accompany the necessary workman, for he wants to take
advantage of the two hours required by the operation
to take care of an urgent errand: to inform the police,
at the closest station, of the attack made upon him
this morning at dawn.

The locksmith is an old man, bald and myopic, who
does not seem disturbed in the slightest by the little
raindrops still falling, now that the worst of the
shower is past, on the shoulders of his jacket and on
his gleaming skull. Carefully he introduces a metal
blade into the lock, which he then turns very gently,
listening, his ear almost pressed against the door, to
the tiny noises caused by the possible contacts with
the parts it touches, in order to discern their hidden
nature. As a matter of fact, the customer, as usual
under such circumstances, was unable to describe,
even roughly, the shape and arrangement of the
notches on the lost key.

It is his eye, now, that the man applies to the tiny
opening; then there are new metal blades, selected deliberately from the toolbox. There must be something
that disturbs him, for he looks through the keyhole
again, trying to illuminate the interior of the mecha-

nism with a cylindrical pocket flashlight, bringing the rounded, luminous tip close to the mysterious and recalcitrant orifice.

But the flashlight, to perform its function, would have to be where his eye is, which is not possible, since in that case there would no longer be anyone there to see; therefore the locksmith soon abandons this attempt and takes another look, without the help of any artificial light. He then notices that the other end of the channel is free and that a bulb is on in the room on the other side of the door, contrary to what would be normal since the house is supposed to be empty. In that case, wouldn't it be enough to ring, in order— once the door was opened—to take the lock apart in order to reconstruct a new key as easily as possible?

However, the short bald man is interrupted in the midst of his logical reflections by the exceptional interest of the scene visible to him, on the other side of the door, so that he cannot carry further his analysis of the situation and of the consequences it implies . . . There is a young girl in there lying on the ground, bound and gagged. Judging from the coppery hue of her skin and her thick head of hair, long, smooth and lustrous, with blue highlights in its black abundance, she must be a half-caste girl with a good deal of Indian blood. Her face seems attractive, her features regular, at least insofar as can be gathered apart from the interference of the white silk gag (a scarf tied behind her head) which distorts the mouth, sawing into the corners of the lips. Her hands are tied behind her back, and half-hidden by her position. Her ankles are tied together, one above the other, by means of a thick cord which is wound several times around the long, slightly bent legs, coiling higher up around the belly and hips, then imprisoning the arms and the chest by many interlacing spirals, pulled very tight as is indicated by the indentations made in the flesh at the least resistant points: the breasts, the waist, the thighs.

There has been a struggle, judging from appearances, or in any case the girl must have attempted to evade capture, for her bright red dress is in great disorder, though now immobilized as well by the cord. The skirt, a rather short one it is true, rises on one side to the pubic area, thereby revealing a wide zone of bare skin above the embroidered stocking, while the blouse has been torn far down over one shoulder, where the flesh glistens under the harsh light from a tall lamp with a Chinese shade set on the nearby table.

It is toward this lamp, struggling sideways as much as her fetters permit, that the prisoner raises eyes widened by terror, or perhaps only by her prone and half-overturned position. She is apparently trying to prop herself up on one elbow, but not very successfully because of the cords which keep her from moving her arm. Beside her, on the floor, in close proximity to her bare shoulder, is an indefinable black shape which looks like a small-size leather glove, without cuff, the fingers worn and spread every which way. As has been said, the dark-skinned girl pays no attention to this last detail, the point which attracts her horrified and eager glances being located in a direction almost diametrically opposite: the careful preparations being made by the second person who figures in the field of vision.

This person is sitting at the table—a man in a white coat with a severe face and gray hair, wearing steel-rimmed glasses. Everything in his features and stature alike has a stereotyped look about it, without real life, without human expression except for that purely conventional hardness and indifference; unless the only thing that gives him this determined aspect is the excessive, exclusive interest he is paying to his experiment. He is in the process, as a matter of fact, in the zone of bright light cast by the lampshade, of inserting a serum (a narcotic or hallucinogenic substance, a nervous stimulant, a poison of either slow or immediate effect) into a hypodermic syringe, his left hand holding the tapering cylindrical shaft which ends in a slender hollow needle, point upward, while he maneuvers between the thumb and forefinger of his other hand the round tip of the glass piston-valve. Behind his glasses, whose lenses cast stylized reflections, he watches the level of the liquid with the care required of high-precision measurements.

Nothing, in the scene, permits identification of the exact nature, or even the expected effect, of this colorless fluid whose injection requires such a setting and causes so much anxiety to the young captive. The uncertainty as to the precise meaning of the episode is all the greater in that the title of the work is missing, the upper part of the cover, where it would normally be found, having been torn across and removed, deliberately or not.

I ask Laura where the book comes from.

"It was there," she answers with a vague gesture toward the room with empty shelves behind her. And her gaze is direct, motionless, absent.

"That's strange," I say, "I've never seen it before . . ."

"It was lying flat on one of the top shelves, in a corner."

"I see . . . What made you think of looking for it up there?"

"I just happened to look."

"Didn't you have to use a ladder?"

"No. I climbed up on the shelves, step by step."

She has to be lying. The notion of any such scene, as I try in vain to imagine it, is too preposterous.

Or else perhaps it is true, in spite of everything. Each time I ask this kind of question, which soon turns into an interrogation, she always has the same slow, precise, remote diction, as if she were reciting her answers in a dream or in the voice—perceptible to herself alone—of an oracle. But at the same time, her tone does not permit the least objection: it is clear that, in her mind, the facts leave no room for ulterior motives. She also gives the impression, to some degree, of having on her side the guarantee of slide rule, by means of which she has just discovered and announced the sole solution to the problem set.

I take refuge in my turn in the pages of the book, which I leaf through, pretending to be interested in the adventures of the characters. From what I can guess, the lovely half-caste in the garish picture is named Sara. She is the possessor of three terrible secrets, related each to the other, which she has sworn never to give away, their triple revelation bound to unleash irreparable catastrophes for herself as well as for the whole world. Her fear is so great that one day or another she will betray some scrap of a story by which her tormented mind is obsessed, that she lives locked up in her own house, where only the family physician visits every evening, caring for her since the dramatic disappearance of all her family. But she has told nothing to this good-humored old man, who is pained to see such a lovely girl living in this incomprehensible imprisonment. He decides therefore to call in, without asking his patient's permission, a fake analyst—a man named Morgan—who is undertaking, unknown to him, the investigation of the girl's buried past, in order to determine the origin of the disturbances which her behavior seems to reveal.

This man is doubtless the one in the white coat, and his syringe would therefore contain a truth serum which he is preparing, as a last resort, to inject into the body, at the top of the thigh whose tender flesh he has managed to expose by squeezing the cords over the dress. Sara's anguish thereby would derive from her conviction, imprisoned as she is in the labyrinth of her sick mind, that her tongue will immediately begin betraying, from beginning to end, the forbidden narrative which is burning her lips. One sudden detail disturbs me: it is said in passing that the girl in question has blue eyes, which does not at all fit in with the general coloring, of skin or hair, attributed by the artist to the victim in the illustration adorning the cover.

But what strikes me even more now, in the crudely colored drawing, is that the dark shape with complicated outlines like those of an ink blot shown on the floor is not a woman's glove as I had thought originally, but a huge spider with hairy legs which is crawling toward the captive's bare shoulder and neck. Is this creature part of the experiment, or does it play a separate role, no one having yet noticed its presence? (To be specific: no one except me, which is to say, neither Sara nor Doctor Morgan, for I have noticed, in skimming the novel, that of the three elements of the secret in the heroine's keeping, one was known by the reader, the second by the narrator himself, and the third by the book's author alone.) While I am making these various observations, I keep trying at the same time (though as yet without results) to wedge into my memory the notion of Laura climbing up the library shelves without having had—she says— any specific reason for doing so; this image seems to me more and more absurd and impossible, unless the child was frightened by a giant spider or by a rat: if it was the noise of broken glass, at one of the windows at the end of the corridor, which had caused her panic, she would have been more likely to look for a hiding-place in some closet or even in a bathroom, but she would not have climbed up to the top of the shelves . . .

At this moment, while I am still looking in the book, leafing through the pages almost at random, for the one which would correspond to the illustration, in order to verify the exact circumstances of the injection and to elucidate the possible help, or on the contrary the change made by this creature in the course of the experiment, I once again fall upon the passage in which the narrator, disguised as a policeman, bursts into the apartment of the young redhead known as Joan.

The man has come to a stop a few steps away from his victim, contemplating with interest her naked body, with the exception—as has been said—of the green leather shoes, the black stockings with the pink lace garters, and the tiny gold cross . . . But now I begin to have a certain qualm: if I recognize this fragment textually (and not only anecdotally, for that would prove nothing, analogous situations are to be found in most novels on sale in the pornographic bookshops of Times Square), then this volume, whose cover I have forgotten, has already passed before my eyes. It is therefore pointless to torment Laura about her so-called recent acquisition. And, once again, I tell myself that she is leading a sad and unhealthy life in this house, without projects, without surprises, without a possible future.

For a long time now, she has lost all real communication with the outside world, to which she now has only artificial links, constituted for the most part— aside from the fragments of personal memories whose most violent scenes I hope I have made her forget—by this detective-story library in decay, by the ordinary anecdotes which I myself supply to her, carefully expurgating from them any allusion to destructive episodes, and finally, at certain hours and on condition that she take the usual precautions when she half-opens the curtains in her room, by the playground of the school where, behind a heavy wire fence at least six yards high, the black girls play like all children, performing what appear to be cruel and mysterious rites.

I, too, should be making an effort to entertain my little prisoner more, since I have decided (temporarily?) to keep her with me, well protected, in order to shield her from the supreme decisions and to guard her from harm. Not to mention the fact that if she gets too bored, Laura might some day, in my absence, commit a monstrous crime which will destroy us both. But what can I be thinking of? In any case, I would have to renew her stock of criminal cases; the selection would be easy enough from the windows of the bookstores specializing in such matters, since the image on the cover plays such a great part in the interest awakened by these works. I could also bring her candy, books of erotic photographs, perfume, fashion magazines, comic books, marijuana cigarettes, and perhaps install a television set: color newsreels would do something to change the atmosphere of this three-quarters unfurnished building which serves as her prison, and would however inadequately remedy the early interruption of her studies by the documentary films on Africa or the Far East.

As for bringing her playmates, there could be no question of that, unfortunately, unless I were to choose as guests—different, therefore, on each occasion—the young women who figure on the execution lists: to lure them here on some pretext, to leave them with Laura long enough for her to divert herself with them, and to keep in readiness the necessary arrangements for their sacrifice, either on the spot or elsewhere, without these victims being able, meanwhile, to make contact with anyone whether or not he (or she) belongs to the organization. If their torture were to take place right here, moreover, it is possible that Laura would develop a taste for it, at least as a spectator.

I noted just now that I would return on some occasion to another important point: to try to give a more precise description of the way in which she expresses herself when I ask her a question, or when she tells me about her day, when I return in the evening. Her words never form a continuous discourse: they are like fragments which nothing any longer links together, despite the emphatic tone suggesting a coherent whole which might exist somewhere, elsewhere than in her head probably; and there is always, suspended above the elements stuck together one way or another, the apprehension of an imminent, unforeseeable though ineluctable catastrophe which will reduce this precarious order to nothingness.

And finally, exhausted by calculating everything, I end up by waiting in my turn for the incalculable event which is going to make everything blow up in another moment. And so I return to the house, night after night, and set down my key on the marble table top in the vestibule, and I climb the staircase step after step, with all the weight of the day's accumulated fatigue in my legs. And I listen, ears cocked, for some sound that might still be coming from her room. And if I were to justify disobedience to my orders by some impulse of uncontrolled passion, it would be very hard for me to swear in good faith that her illicit possession affords me, in the long run, more pleasure than anxiety. But these regrets, these hesitations, are scarcely appropriate, for meanwhile the narrative I have begun continues its course up near Harlem, in the overheated apartment on One Hundred and Twenty-third Street where the fake policeman tells Joan she has just been sentenced to death by the parallel court of special jurisdiction and that, as is traditional in such cases, he will first have to torture her at some length in order to make her confess the details of the conspiracy. Moreover he intends, he says, to acquit himself of this task conscientiously, for he will take great pleasure in it, as she can suspect, the wearing of a military tunic and boots scarcely preventing a man from having human feelings. To such a degree that the time will not be wasted, even in the considerable likelihood that she will ultimately have nothing to tell that the police do not know already.

This last declaration must constitute, in the soldier's mind, a kind of polite homage to his victim's perfect beauty, for he accompanies the phrase with a discreet salute: a nod in her direction, a little stiff but very worldly. Unaffected by this attention, under the circumstances, the young woman, who still holds her hands above her auburn hair falling in loose curls of a delightful (or provocative) disarray, the young woman steps back toward the sheet of glass, widening still further her green eyes filled with panic (or terror, or stupor, etc.).

"I see that you have already prepared some instruments," the man adds with a faint smile, keeping the barrel of his gun aimed at the captive, and at the same time making a movement with his head toward the ironing-board, the gleaming sharp-pointed scissors, and the electric iron which is beginning to smoke on the silk dress. He decides, at the same time, that the board, too, will be useful: it has a very practical elongated shape and its metal legs, which diverge toward the floor, afford it a good stability; they are even provided, at about the lower third, with four little leather thongs which seem ideal for tying up the victim's wrists and ankles. The policeman even wonders what else they could be used for. On the point of asking the doomed girl this question, he changes his mind, glancing back toward her.

"I shall begin by raping you," he says. "I shall doubtless do so again during the course of the interrogation, as is recommended in our instructions, but I want to take you first, before I tie you up. That

79

television program has worked me up a little, although in our profession, I can tell you, we see a great deal more than that. I have noticed, when I was on the balcony, that the good parts excited you as well; consequently, you may even take a certain interest in what you are going to suffer, at least at first, and I am glad of that, for your sake. (For me, as a matter of fact, as you have understood, the pleasure experienced by the partner plays no part in my personal fixations and fetishes.) Now, get over there, on the divan.

"No, not like that, on your knees. That's better: facing the wall. Lean on your forearms. Bend your head: very nice. Now arch your hips a little. Open your thighs wider. Now arch your hips more—as much as you can. There! You really do have as good a body as they say; your skin is very delicate, to look at as well as to touch, and you smell very pleasant. All of which, moreover, figures in the report. All right, you little whore, no more airs: remember that this is a kind of reprieve after all, and soon you'll be regretting how easy it was, despite these contacts that seem to shock you and the posture you now regard as uncomfortable.

"Good. That's better. We can get on with the preliminary questions right away, if you're ready. When you have nothing more to declare, your torture will begin, to see whether or not you have told the truth. Without changing your position nor tying you up any more than now, we can first of all, for purely plastic reasons, send a little blood over these white buttocks of yours. Then, when we turn you over (chiefly, of course, to deal with the breasts and the vulva) it will be better to tie you securely to the ironing-board. I hope that you will then, in fact, have nothing else

very interesting to say, for I shall have to turn the television volume up to its maximum point, in order to
drown out your screams, so that I shall no longer understand your answers.

"Oh, I almost forgot: between the two parts of the
program, you will have to give me something to drink
and serve me a snack—ham and eggs will do, for
example. You will behave, during this intermission,
attentively and considerately. You can even make conversation with me, as you smoke your last cigarette; it
would be in your own interest, at least, to extend this
respite as long as possible. Afterward, in any case,
whether or not you add some new detail under the
effect of pain, you will be tortured to death, as is provided for in your sentence. Don't bother to protest,
it's pointless. And save your tears: the bleating of the
lamb, says a Chinese proverb, merely arouses the tiger.
Let's see now, your name is Joan Robeson. Answer, it
will go better for you: as long as you can answer, you
won't have to suffer too seriously. So then, your name
is Robeson?"

"Yes."

"Given name?"

"Joan."

"Nickname?"

"JR."

"How old are you?"

"Twenty-one."

"Profession?"

"Student."

"Of what?"

"History of religion."

"Have you other diplomas?"

"Yes, two."

"In what?"

"Political philosophy. Aesthetics of crime."

"What are your means of subsistence?"

"I work part-time."

"What kind of work?"

"Prostitution."

"Which category?"

"Luxury."

"On your own or for a company?"

"For a company."

"Which company? You'll have to answer more readily, without forcing me to pursue the interrogation at every word. Remember what I have told you! And hold the pose better than that. We were saying: for a company."

"Yes. Johnson Limited. I beg your pardon."

"That's better. But don't move so much, please. Do you like it?"

"Do I like what?"

"Johnson Limited, of course!"

"Yes. They're fair."

"How much do you make?"

"From eighty to a thousand dollars a night. The company takes fifty per cent."

"You must have a tendency to conceal a share of your profits—don't you?"

"No. I'm honest. And in any case, there are the pay slips. They keep a very close watch. Right now, almost everything is automatic: the customers pay more and more with checks made out by a time clock."

"That must be very complicated, with the various services and charges—is it?"

"We have a punch card to make it easier for the machine to work it out."

"You're sure you never cheat?"

"I swear it."

"Good. We'll see in a little while if the tiny pliers of the regulation tool kit, or the long red-hot needles, will make you change your mind. You have gas here, of course?"

"Yes, in the kitchen. Is the question about declaring tips so important?"

"No question is important. Merely a matter of principle. You've read our motto above the visor on our caps: 'Truth, My One Passion'."

"But what if the torture is so intense it makes me tell a lie?"

"That often happens; always, in fact; you'll see, when we insist long enough."

"Then the goal of the operation eludes you, if not the pleasure, doesn't it?"

"No. And don't try to catch me in your specious arguments, in the hope no doubt of escaping the fate which lies in store for you. The case you mention has been foreseen, you are a fool not to have realized that. Let us suppose that at first you claimed one thing, then its contrary; the total of the two answers thus surely includes the expression of the truth in half of the cases. Starting from this certainty, all the rest is no more than a matter of mathematical calculations, performed by the electronic brain to which we shall feed your testimony. It is for this very reason, in order not to distort the results of the calculation, that we must make the torture last as long as possible: thus each assertion will finally be accompanied by its contrary. Do you understand? Good. Now, back to Johnson Limited. Fifty per cent is too much—wouldn't you rather work for the police?"

"In the same line of work?"

"Of course. You seem quite gifted. When I began to caress you, you were already quite moist."

"It must have been on account of that film where the girls were being impaled, or else it was fear, or the sight of a uniform. But if I change employers, I have to give notice. And besides, everything depends on the conditions you can offer."

"We can talk about that more calmly during our rest. First of all, you would be saving your own life, which is an advantage; after only an hour or two of torture for the sake of the rules: that will give you time to think about it, and I won't have come here for nothing. Meanwhile, tell me who Ben-Saïd is."

"Do you know him?"

"The name has come up several times in the report."

"In my opinion, he's nothing much."

"What does he do in your organization?"

"He's a go-between. He's only an Arab, as you know, but our people don't want to show any preferences between one color and another."

"You yourself—are you Jewish?"

"No, of course not: I'm a black girl from Puerto Rico."

"My compliments. I'd never have guessed. So this Ben-Saïd?"

"The chief found him during a fight with the mounted police. For a man like that, it's really a pity wasting his time in such demonstrations; he's very cultivated—he speaks twenty-three languages, including Gaelic and Afrikaans."

"But not English?"

"No. It's not an indispensable dialect for an American revolutionary. In the service, in any case, Spanish is enough . . . You're hurting me, when you do that."

"Yes. I know I am. I want to. What is his specific function?"

"Go-between. I've already answered that question."

"Why did you say he was nothing much?"

"Oh, a lot of reasons. One day they sent him to watch a house down in the Village where something funny was going on, though it is supposed to be inhabited by one of our agents. Ben-Saïd came in the obvious outfit of a private detective, with a plastic mask clumsily put on, dark glasses and the whole get-up: a hat with the brim turned down, black raincoat with the collar turned up, and so on. And in that kind of disguise, he started playing sentry on the sidewalk across the street . . ."

"All right. We have that passage in the file already. The only point I wasn't sure of, is that the man was Ben-Saïd. Can you give another example?"

"Of course it's Ben-Saïd! Just take a good look at him when you go home tonight. Under the mask, he still has that nervous tic in his left cheek; and after a while the plastic of the mask makes a diagonal wrinkle between the cheekbone and the nostril. It makes him feel he has to keep pulling at the lower edge to keep everything together; since he's afraid this gesture will give the game away, he keeps his hands deep in his pockets, which only emphasizes the fact that he's a cop—it's ridiculous. Sorry. Just now, before the three of us were beginning to put the cigarettes in the Buick, I thought he was a plain-clothes man from a distance and I almost went on my way instead of stopping the car where I was supposed to: I was sure the plan had been given away. It was just at the last minute, driving very slowly along the curb as if I was cruising, that I recognized Ben-Saïd. I kidded him a little when we got out, and after that he sulked during the job, you remember . . ."

"I asked you for another example in support of your opinion of the man, not your trivial personal stories with regard to your life as a salesgirl in a department store or a part-time secretary."

"Oh please, don't do that any more. I can't stand it. I beg your forgiveness. You'll see. I promise to be nice. I'll do whatever you want. And I won't mention those things again, since you don't want me to."

"Don't move so much, or I'll tie you up right away. And try to invent details that will be exact and meaningful."

"Yes. Oh please, don't do that. The subway. There, that's it: the subway car and the scene with the three hoodlums in leather jackets. Ben-Saïd is riding, in the middle of the night, in an empty car hurtling on the express track to some other borough—Brooklyn, I think—the time and place where there are always young punks who spend their time riding from one end of the line to the other looking for some dirty trick they can play. I've been mugged often enough myself on that line, coming home from work. It's a bad scene, because if you don't give them what they want, they tie your hands behind your back and then, after having taken turns with you, they hang you to a luggage rack or else they toss you out an open window onto the track, sometimes they leave you tied to the train by a rope so that the train goes on its way without the conductor noticing anything, which tears off all your clothes, mutilates the body, breaks all the limbs and inflicts so many wounds that the corpse is unidentifiable when it gets to the next station. I've had several friends killed that way. But if on the contrary, to avoid that, you let them do what they want with you, you risk a session with the union for clandestine professional activities. The fine is so high that you have to spend the rest of your life paying it; not to mention the fact that you can even be dealing with an *agent provocateur:* that also happened to a girl I work with at the office . . . No, oh please, don't do that. I thought you would like it if I changed the subject. But now I'll go back to Ben-Saïd. He is sitting in his corner, facing the way the train is going, in the front of the car, and because of all the racket the express trains make, he doesn't hear the young hoodlums who have come in at the other end of the car, and who are plotting behind him, deciding what it will be best to do. They are kids of about fifteen, all three the same height, but on closer examination, it is clear that one of them is a girl, although her clothes—tight pants and black leather jacket—are exactly the same, in principle, as those of the other two. A slender girl, though clearly past puberty, with a graceful figure and cropped blond hair. You can see that her clothes are not mass-produced: their style is elegant, the materials soft, not too shiny, probably expensive; the pants are black leather too, with a zipper like the jacket, whose collar is open far down her chest—you can see where her breasts begin. It is so hot in the subways that the girls usually have nothing underneath. Yes, all right, I'm going on. The two boys, who are also blond, have regular faces with rather fine features, despite their somewhat effeminate style, the extreme negligence of their clothes, cigarette in the corner of the mouth, hair too long, etc. One of the two is especially filthy; his denim pants—gray rather than black, are torn about six inches above the left ankle, as if it had caught on a barbed wire during some robbery; and his shoes, whose laces cannot come untied because of the knots holding the broken pieces together, are worn like slippers, the counters broken down deliberately. His way of talking does not seem to be the reflection of very extensive study.

Moreover, it appears to be the girl who gives the orders. She even wears, on her left shoulder, a gold bar which at first glance looks like a lieutenant's insignia; at closer range it is apparent that the gold line is not continuous but instead a series of capital letters in heavy type forming a name: LAURA. The boys have only their initial embroidered in red on the right pocket of their jackets, which helps distinguish them from each other, for otherwise, in face and figure, except for the extreme dirtiness of the one, they could be mistaken for identical twins. The embroidered letters are an M for the dirtier one, a W for his brother. Their entire given names must be written on the identity bracelets they each wear on their right wrist, but the engraved surface is turned in toward the skin, and the heavy nickel chain is twisted.

The girl has determined the plan of attack: it is W (whose general appearance is slightly more respectable) who is sent alone, as a lure, to this solitary and exhausted traveler, though he is dressed in a style which indicates wealth and, doubtless, special tastes as well. (Ben-Saïd abandoned his raincoat that day in favor of a camel's-hair overcoat, this outfit completed by a snap-brimmed felt hat.) Meanwhile, the other boy and Laura return to the next car. Since this car is also empty, the girl decides that her companion should take advantage of the fact. Therefore, to encourage him, she takes the occasion of a sharper jolt, around a curve of the track, to let herself slump against the—supposedly—male chest, clinging to the boy's hips on the excuse of regaining her own balance. This contact is all the more interesting for her partner in that the zipper which controls the opening of the girl's jacket has slid another few inches lower in the course of this slight movement, so that the slit has now reached her navel, whose flower-shaped depression appears between the two rows of tiny metal teeth, at the very tip of a slender V of bare skin. The gesture has been so regular, so prompt and so natural that it might seem to be a pure accident, or on the other hand an exercise repeated many times over. The boy has no need of further explanations, and without bothering to elucidate this last problem, he grasps his lieutenant with a firm arm around the waist—still to keep her from falling—then, having removed the cigarette from between his lips with his other hand, he presses his mouth against the girl's, which is just at the right height. Feeling that his kiss is being returned warmly, eagerly, passionately, etc., he drops the cigarette butt to the floor and slips his now free hand into the opening of the jacket.

Everything seems to be going well—since the slender tip of the nipple is already rising (or else stiffening, extending, swelling, hardening, bulging, becoming erect, turgescent, etc., the point is made) under the caress of three filthy fingers, while lower down, a faintly swelling triangle of soft black leather begins rubbing against the rough gray grease-stained trousers

—when, suddenly, the girl pulls away her lips, steps back with a sudden gesture which liberates both her waist and her breast, and violently slaps her abashed partner, in order to teach him to respect his superiors in rank. And immediately, with a prim gesture of outraged modesty, she pulls the large brass ring of the zipper up to her neck, hermetically sealing the jacket with a hiss of torn cloth, or the whisper of a whip over the naked flesh, a sigh of the air in the throat when the lungs inhale too quickly under the effect of pain, the silky sound of the long wound opened by the tip of the knife, the scratch of the match against its striking surface, the sudden crackle, in the flames, of fine lace lingerie, of loose hair, of the hank of auburn silk, or of the burning bush, or of the golden fleece, that will do, you may go on.

Motionless and teeth clenched, six feet away from the boy bending down to pick up his extinguished cigarette butt and, once he has straightened up, replacing it in the corner of his mouth, Laura stares with a shrug of repugnance at the bulging fly of the tight denim trousers. A scornful or mocking smile, or a sneer of satisfied curiosity, passes over her closed lips and between the long lashes of her half-closed eyes, then she declares in her best Cambridge accent: "Oh, Mark-Anthony, you are disgusting!" At the same moment, the two accomplices burst out into a brief childish laugh; then, holding hands at a reasonable distance, they perform up and down the empty car an improvised dance on Sioux themes.

But a second later, they are once again motionless and rigid, facing each other. The boy must have lit his cigarette butt again, for from it rises, as before, a slender twisting thread of smoke. After an indeterminate period of time, without even removing the butt stuck in the corner of his mouth, he expectorates a clear, round wad of spit against the windowpane, behind which are passing the dim empty platforms of a local station. Laura, staring at the blob of heavy whitish saliva whose lower edge is beginning to dribble toward the bottom of the pane, notices on the other side of the glass the equidistant, identical, numberless examples of a giant poster repeated at brief intervals, from end to end of the dilapidated curving white ceramic-tile wall: the huge face of a young woman whose eyes are covered by a black bandage and whose lips are parted. Insofar as the speed of the train makes it possible to judge, this poster must be a good reproduction of a color photograph, with pastel shades, whose relief stands out very clearly against a rather dark background. Just below a delicately outlined chin can be read a cursive script and alone decipherable of the probably brief text of this advertisement, the word: "Tomorrow . . ." On the last poster of the series, at the end of the platform, someone has added to the series, with a skillful hand reproducing the same shape of letters and the same spacing, but in red paint instead of the sky-blue of the printed letters: "The Revolution."

Then it is the dark tunnel again, and the pale reflection of the boy's face which slides parallel to the train along the rough cement wall, a little higher than the festoon of three cables, one above the next. But the wall, so close that it could almost be touched by a hand thrust out of the open space between the cars, suddenly moves away and vanishes: the light cast by the illuminated train no longer falls on any lateral obstacle, as if the empty cars were henceforth hurtling

91

through the complete void of the night. At the same time the noise has abruptly altered: the racket of the wheels on the rails, the creaking of the axles, the vibration of the metal sheets, have lost their proximity, their immediate aggressiveness; but, echoed by a higher vault which thus betrays its invisible existence, at a distance of several dozen yards or more, the sound has increased in volume: magnified, filled with deep overtones and successive echoes which multiply its power, as if it were being retransmitted by means of a hundred loudspeakers, it drowns out everything this time with its diffuse but deafening, monstrous presence, which fills the gigantic subterranean cavity, the interior of the car, the ears, even the skull, last chamber of resonance in which are concentrated the hammerings and rumblings of the metal.

And I, meanwhile, in the mounting racket of the metal carcass vibrating under my hurrying steps, continue down the endless and dizzying fire escape. At each new landing, I interrupt my descent a second to lean over the railing and I perceive below me, still a little farther away, the mute, anxious crowd, perhaps already hundreds of yards distant, so remote that the raised faces now constitute only a sea of white specks.

Then I close the book with the torn cover and return it to its preceding reader after glancing one last time at the illustration, whose exact meaning still escapes me; it seems to me that the spider, on the floor, has again perceptibly advanced toward the bare shoulder. But now Laura suddenly begins telling me a story which, she says, has taken up some of her afternoon. Despite a suddenly animated, even amused tone, she still gives that impression of receiving from elsewhere her ready-made sentences, whose meaning she herself can decipher only in the course of speaking them aloud. According to the story, she heard noises on the doorstep, at the door, and managed to approach their source along the vestibule wall: someone was poking into the lock. She soon realized that it was some maniac, whose goal was not to open the door but to see through the keyhole: by standing on tiptoe and keeping in the dark, standing obliquely against the rectangular pane protected outside by a heavy design of cast-ironwork, she saw the bald head of the man bent down in the posture of a voyeur, though the spaces between the volutes of the cast-iron grille, a little higher, gave him many more opportunities to see something inside, and with much less trouble.

At first Laura had thought of putting out his eye with a knitting needle, but then something much more amusing occurred to her, thanks in fact to that detective story she had been reading and was holding in her hand at that moment. After having torn off the upper part of the cover, for the presence of the title and the author's name risks destroying the illusion, she sets the image just opposite the tiny keyhole, at the right distance so that the observer outside can see the subject as a whole, but not the edges of the paper. When everything is ready, she switches on the light, pressing the button within reach of her hand, while holding the book quite still.

Since the locksmith is nearsighted, he does not notice that the scene is quite close, entirely fixed and flat; he imagines it life-size and located much farther away: at the end of a corridor. The suspended gesture of the man carefully adjusting the needle of the syringe still allows for the possibility of coming to the rescue of his unfortunate victim who is about to have paraffin injected into her veins. He has come in time. Without bothering to make out the details of the scene, he rushes off to get help, abandoning his tools on the doorstep.

The false Ben-Saïd, in the recess of the house across the street, wonders about the reason for such strange behavior, and what the man can have seen through the keyhole. However, no order permits him to leave his post to look for himself: it might be a trick, and while he was trying to discover something which does not exist, his eye glued to the door, someone would signal from the windows to an accomplice outside. Therefore the sentry merely takes out of an inside pocket a tiny black notebook whose imitation-leather covers are so worn that they show the underlying fabric at the corners; then, after removing his gloves and thrusting them under his left armpit, he writes down, according to his previous observations, the succinct narrative of the occurrence, as well as the exact time, down to the second according to his wrist watch. In the effort he is making to make his task both brief and exact, a nervous tic produces, on two occasions, a wrinkle across his left cheek. Then, without thinking about it, still preoccupied by the sentence whose composition has given him so much difficulty, he puts the notebook back in his pocket and immediately afterward, taking between both thumbs and forefingers the loose flesh of his neck on either side of his chin, he pulls at his skin in hopes of controlling this involuntary twitching which disturbs him, a little as if he were trying to replace a poorly applied plastic mask.

Laura, who has heard the voyeur's footsteps hurrying down the steps outside and fading away down the sidewalk to the right, has put out the light and once again approached the glass peephole, in order to examine the street. The man in black having put his gloves back on and his hands back in his pockets, she leaves her observation post and takes a few vague steps toward the staircase. No brief smile passes over her pursed lips nor between the long lashes of her eyelids. Having reached the table, she ceremoniously makes the gesture of setting down on its marble top a bunch of imaginary keys, while glancing up toward the big mirror. Her face withdrawn, her eyes wide and blank, she stares at herself blindly a moment, in the watery depths of the vestibule poorly lit by the half-light from the rectangular opening in the door. After a considerable interval of complete immobility and silence, she says half-aloud the word "ulva" which floats into her mind from somewhere or other.

Noticing her own reflection at this moment, she tries to reproduce the twitch of the cheek she has just observed once again in the figure wearing the black raincoat. She succeeds and takes advantage of the occasion to experiment with several other rapid and periodic grimaces, affecting various portions of the face. Then she utters two more words, a little more loudly and with exaggerated lip movements: "Axial sex," followed after a rather long pause, during which her cheek has twitched three times in a row, by the uncompleted sentence: ". . . the body lying on the steps of the altar, with the seven knives planted in the flesh, around the auburn fleece . . ." which derives from the popular novel with the torn cover, which is now under her left arm. Finally, still with as much deliberation and seriousness as before, she says: "Don't forget to set fire to it, Mark-Anthony."

She then notices, in the mirror, the half-open door

of the library; she quickly turns around toward the actual object and enters the room with careful, silent steps, as if she were hoping to surprise someone there. But no one is there, and it is easy to determine as much at first glance, for there is no furniture either, except for the empty shelves which cover the walls all the way up to the ceiling. Laura takes the book she had put under her arm, at the same time as Ben-Saïd's black gloves, and flings it toward the upper shelf, in the darkest corner, for its role is now over and done with.

She mounts the staircase step by step, making herself feel, in her own young legs, all the exhaustion accumulated during a long, nonexistent day of work. At the first landing, she drops her key inadvertently; the complicated noise the key makes as it knocks against one of the iron bars of the railing, then landing on the imitation-stone floor, resembles—does not resemble—the sharp clatter of a pane of glass broken by a murderer breaking the window at the end of the corridor.

At the end of the corridor, the cracked pane is still in place, indicated in the glass surface only by a fourteen-branched star covering its entire surface, no piece of which has as yet been removed. Several of the rays of the star—five, precisely, or perhaps six—stop before having reached the edges of the pane; it would be tempting to make them continue by pressing lightly against the central point, but the risk of breaking the pane altogether is too great; especially since the fragments which would fall outside, onto the fire escape, would immediately attract the attention of the jailer keeping watch on the opposite sidewalk.

He is now as motionless as a wax dummy, the kind

to be seen in police museums. Laura, crouching against the French window, has already been staring at him for a moment, the line of her gaze passing between two strips of the fire-escape landing. It would certainly be amusing to make him look up by breaking a windowpane or by doing something else, then, slowly rising a few inches, to show on a level with the platform, between the vertical bars of the railing, a grimacing head of a decapitated girl.

But Laura's right hand happens to encounter, as it changes its position, one of the pieces of glass which has fallen onto the floor. Resting one knee on the tiles, at a place carefully chosen in order not to cut herself, her chin on the other knee and her lips caressing the taut smooth skin sliding beneath the tip of her tongue, the girl begins gathering up, between two meticulous fingers, the slender transparent daggers and collecting them one by one in the hollow of her other palm, very slowly, as deliberately and with as many precautions and as much respect as if they were diamonds.

When she stands up again and looks down the long corridor in front of her, with all the doors which open to the right and left, she no longer manages to remember which leads to her own room, where she must go, however, in order to put in safekeeping the crystal knives she has just made for herself. All the doors are identical and there seem to be more of them than usual. Laura bends over against the first one to try and see, through the keyhole, what is on the other side; but she sees nothing, and she dares not continue because of the short bald man's knitting needle. She pushes open the door suddenly, violently. The door knocks against a rubber stop and returns, quivering, to a half-open position. The room is empty: neither murderer nor bed nor furniture of any kind. Laura moves on to the next.

At the fifth door, she finds herself in another room without any furniture, so that it is still not hers, yet which must be since it overlooks in the same way the courtyard surrounded with high fences of a girls' school, moreover the same one probably. The students are at recess; however there do not seem to be very many today: six in all, playing some kind of blind-man's buff. These little girls—as usual, with rare exceptions—are all blacks, about twelve to fourteen years old. It is one of the youngest who is wearing the white silk bandage over her eyes and who moves about uncertainly, timidly, her arms extended in front of her, exploring the air like the antennae of a blind insect, and her lips parted. The other five who surround her are each furnished with a long steel T square which doubtless is part of the drawing-kit they must use to produce geometrical figures in their class notebooks. But their function here is actually that of banderilleros in the bull ring. As they advance and retreat to remain two or three steps away from their unarmed playmate, which is to say out of reach of her hands which are nonetheless timorous rather than threatening, they slowly perform around her a kind of wild dance, taking great silent steps, making broad gestures with their arms above their heads, sweeping and ceremonious salutations which, without any apparent or even symbolic meaning, seem nonetheless to belong to the ritual of some religious sacrifice. From time to time, one or the other comes up and roughly touches, with the end of her T square, the defenseless girl vulnerable to their blows, choosing the sensitive

points carefully enough to make the victim stagger
and even, on occasion, rub the wounded place as
though to assuage the pain.

All this happens without outcry or turbulence of
any kind: it is a mute, mild, almost muffled game, and
the rubber-soled tennis shoes do not make the slightest sound on the cement of the courtyard, across which
the group moves as it circles the victim.

At the relative height of the fence, in relation to the
parallelogram of the courtyard, Laura realizes her
mistake: her own room must be on the floor above.

She therefore returns, walking deliberately, down
the corridor to the staircase over which she leans a
moment, holding on to the railing, her arms stretched
out on either side of her body, bent over almost horizontally, her head to one side, her ear cocked to hear
the missing sounds which would rise from below:
sounds of a key, sounds of a door, sounds of footsteps,
sounds of the pages of a book. Then she resumes her
slow progress up the staircase, step by step, her left
palm and its five outspread fingers encircling the
wooden banister. But, reaching the next landing, she
hears once again quite distinctly, although with the
imagination of memory, the faint knocks audible in
this place from time to time, in reality, coming from
still higher up, from the unoccupied rooms of the top
floor, as if someone were tapping with his finger tips
against a wooden panel, a signal or a gesture of impatience or a long code message transmitted to some
other secret inhabitant of the house.

Laura therefore continues her light, heavy ascent, as
though benumbed, but with an increased circumspec-
tion, this time setting both feet, one after the other,
on each step, the left one first, then the right, avoiding

any shock or friction of her sole, and scarcely touching the railing with her thumb and forefinger to avoid making it creak.

Having reached the top, she walks forward at first, with the same gait of a sleepwalking paralytic, to the French window overlooking the last landing of the fire escape. She notices that the man in the black raincoat—whom she has baptized Ben-Saïd because of a minor character in the book with the torn cover—is now talking to two uniformed policemen wearing flat-topped caps, leather shoulder straps and holstered revolvers. The two men have come to a standstill just at the edge of the roadway, as if some regulation forbade them to leave the darker asphalt altogether. They are standing in exactly the same way, one foot in the gutter and the other resting on the stone curb, thereby resembling—by their identical clothing, corpulence and posture—a single individual doubled by his mirror reflection. The revolver itself completes this illusion, the man on the right having slipped the strap over his left shoulder and the man on the left, over the right shoulder.

There are also, in fact, the two opposite boots which are placed one close to the other, on a slight elevation, the stone curb. The right foot of the man on the left and the left foot of the man on the right are thus arranged in such a manner, side by side and parallel, that they seem to belong to an intermediary figure who would have his left foot on the right and his right foot on the left. But the third figure of the group is actually Ben-Saïd, who has left his recess in order to come over to the gutter, the frontier of the smoother and paler zone of asphalt of which he himself is the guardian. He is standing exactly opposite the inverted boots and thereby presents, contrary to what would be normal if he were dealing with a single interlocutor, his left shoe in front of the left boot and his right shoe in front of the right boot.

He has taken his black-gloved hands out of his pockets and makes a sign toward the right end of the street (hence to his left, although the gesture is performed with his right hand), in other words toward the subway station. Since Laura knows that he is then going to raise his head and look toward the window where she is standing, at the top of the fire escape—according to the action already described—she takes a sudden step back, at the same time that she immediately turns around toward the long corridor.

In order to facilitate her task of inspection, she tries at first to count the doors which open, symmetrically, on each side, opposite each other. She functions calmly and with deliberation. On the right side, there are twelve doors; but then she finds thirteen, counting on the left side. Since the doors are quite regularly arranged in pairs, on each side of the corridor, there must be the same number on each side; hence the number of pairs has increased by one unit between the first count and the second. Laura starts walking and begins checking the empty rooms, one by one, trying to remember the order of each room visited. She walks fast now, although still without making a sound. She opens the door on the right, rapidly inspects the bare walls, closes the door whose ceramic knob is still in her hand, releases the knob, turns around toward the left door which she immediately opens in its turn, again inspects the bare walls, closes the door, walks on twelve steps, opens the right door, inspects the floor and the bare walls, etc.

At the twenty-sixth room, she stops and mentally calculates that she has already taken, down the corridor, a hundred and forty-four steps since the first door. The corridor which still continues in front of her seems to contain at least as many doors, if not more. Yes, many more, on reflection. Laura remains there without moving, her head straight and her body marking its own bilateral symmetry, exactly in the axis of the corridor. This must last quite a long time. Then, still motionless, she begins to scream: a long continuous cry, starting very low, which gradually swells to a paroxysm cut short, whose echo she then listens to as it echoes from one end to the other of the enormous corridor.

From one end to the other of the corridor extends a strip of dazzlingly white carpeting which occupies about a third of the white-tiled floor between the two white walls with their white-lacquered doors. Laura then understands why her footsteps make so little noise. She then continues on her way on the thick carpeting to the next rooms. She puts out her hand toward a new ceramic knob, but interrupts her gesture, her fingers already curled around an imaginary sphere about four inches from the real one.

There is blood, a trickle of thick fresh bright red blood which runs under the door, coming from inside. It forms a kind of tongue about two inches wide, its tip slightly wider where it advances over the tiles, quite slowly but regularly, toward Laura's shoes. At this moment, Laura realizes that she is barefoot, contrary to what she would have supposed. And now a second vermilion trickle appears beside the first one, passing in the same way through the interstice which separates the white-lacquered wood from the ceramic tiles. Then, almost immediately, a third and fourth tongue of blood appear from under the door, framing the first two on the right and the left, but faster than they, more fluid, more abundant, while the earliest is already now on the point of touching Laura's bare foot, resting on the tiles just at the edge of the carpeting which her heel barely touches, an arc tangent to the straight line which constitutes its edge.

Laura carefully draws back her foot. But its shape and position remain indicated on the floor in a red print clearly drawn, with its plantar arch and the tips of the five toes. Yet the trickle of viscous liquid which was advancing toward the big toe was still a few inches away from it. Then had this foot already been walking in the blood? Laura looks up: the ceramic doorknob is also red, as is the inside of the hand slowly turning its palm upward and falling motionless.

At the end of the corridor, down below, out in the street, the false Ben-Saïd then drops his arm, which was indicating to the two men in uniform the subway station (neither policeman moreover has actually looked in this direction), while the real Ben-Saïd is meanwhile still riding, in his yellow imitation-camel's hair overcoat, on an express line which crosses Brooklyn, the only other passenger in his car being a blond adolescent whose black imitation-leather jacket has a W embroidered on one pocket.

The boy has sprawled out indecorously, his legs wide apart and resting only on the tips of his heels on the stained floor, his body leaning back on the wooden bench facing the one on which Ben-Saïd is sitting. But Ben-Saïd is next to the window, whereas the young hoodlum is on the outer side of his bench, having therefore beside him, within reach of his left arm, the little connecting door to the next car, toward the front of the train. In order to attract the attention of this wealthy-looking passenger who seems lost in thought, W puts one hand on the handle behind his shoulder and works it up and down several times, so that the end of the latch slides up each time and falls back into its horizontal position with a heavy click like that of a well-oiled rifle bolt. Ben-Saïd betrays signs of a discreet annoyance (a kind of very faint nervous twitch which periodically convulses the corners of his mouth and his cheek); finally he looks up toward the door, but merely gives a quick, furtive glance at it, moreover a useless one for it was easy enough to guess the origin of the noise. And then he stares down again at the yellow material of his overcoat which is carefully pulled over his knees.

Behind him, at the other end of the car, behind the glass of the other connecting door—in other words, actually, behind two identical and parallel panes of glass, separated by about a yard and belonging to the two corresponding doors of the two adjoining cars linked by a narrow iron platform provided with an iron railing (over which I could easily lean out, as I climb down, in order to glimpse once again the crowd gathered in the street below . . .)—Laura, who is watching the scene and beginning to grow impatient, not understanding why things are not moving faster, makes signs to her accomplice, who is about fifteen yards away. But young W, who cannot readily make out the gestures of his leader or, with all the more reason, her expressions, does not manage to grasp their meaning; since he is afraid of awakening Ben-Saïd's suspicions—although the latter once again keeps his eyes lowered, staring at his thighs, preoccupied by his struggle not to yield to the twitching around his mouth—the youth does not want to risk the slightest communication, even if it were with only one eye, with the girl who, supposing that her signals have not even been seen, indicates her irritation by increasingly nervous gestures, though these are still as difficult to interpret with a view to any action she would thereby be ordering him to perform.

At this moment the subway train stops in an empty station, and Laura sees the man in the yellow overcoat leap up. Even faster, W has raised his left leg to a horizontal position, knee stiff, and has set the heel on the edge of the opposite bench, which blocks Ben-Saïd's way. The three double doors of the car then open simultaneously, operated by the driver at the head of the train, employing a decrepit and noisy remote-control system. But there is no one on the platform, nor does anyone seem to be getting out of the train, in any case out of the cars in the immediate proximity. Ben-Saïd, having vainly tried to shove aside the young hoodlum's leg, decides to use another method, less dignified but more effective: to get past it by climbing over it.

He has scarcely had time to make the necessary movement with one foot than the boy, who had thrust one hand into an inside pocket of his jacket, has pulled it out again holding an object which the passenger can immediately identify as a closed knife, with all the more certainty, moreover, in that it does not remain closed for long: the boy having operated the switchblade mechanism with an expert finger, a shiny, pointed, well-sharpened blade springs out of the ivory handle and comes to rest, threateningly, close to the yellow coat with a click which suggests, more distinctly, the one produced a few seconds earlier by the latch of the little glass door. "Idiot," Laura mutters to herself and concerning not Ben-Saïd but young W who, according to the plans agreed upon, should be using an altogether different system of enticement in order to convince his vis-à-vis to remain in the car with him.

Ben-Saïd hesitates, looks at the knife, the open door to the empty platform, then sidelong at the boy's face in an attempt to assess his determination, stupidity, and criminality, however combined. Unfortunately the young face does not reflect the slightest emotion or disposition of mind or intention of any kind. The double doors slide shut with a long groan, then slam closed, and Ben-Saïd can do nothing but sit down again. As if no murderous intention nor desire to intimidate had ever occurred to him, the boy casually raises his still extended left leg and sets his foot on the floor again, then begins picking his teeth with the point of his knife, a sight so difficult to endure that Ben-Saïd prefers to stare down once again at the synthetic fibers of his overcoat which he carefully rearranges around his knees.

With the same care and the same deliberation, W closes his knife and restores it to the inside pocket of his leather jacket. Then he puts his left hand, close against his shoulder, on the brass handle of the little door between the cars, works the latch and lets it fall back into place with a rifle-like click which makes Ben-Saïd give a start. The passenger stands up and, amazed by the sudden ease of the enterprise, reaches the central corridor in one stride in order to head for the rear of the car. He has just time to notice, at the end, behind the rectangular pane of the little door facing him, Laura's slender, lively figure which immediately stops gesticulating and vanishes to one side, on the metal platform onto which she has stepped during the stop in the empty station.

The train, moving fast again, through a curving tunnel, is now shaken with such sudden jerks that Ben-Saïd must hold onto the nickel-plated vertical bars provided for that purpose. He soon finds himself obliged to sit down, projected by a still more violent jolt onto one of the benches, facing forward as previously but this time in the middle of the car. He wonders if the delicate adolescent girl who was doubtless about to change cars, pursued perhaps by some pervert whose preliminary outrages she has already had to endure, if the delicate adolescent girl with torn underclothes is not going to be thrown now onto the track by one of the jolts, which must be particularly powerful on the narrow jointed platform separating the cars.

The pervert in question, romantically nicknamed "The Subway Vampire" by passengers of the line, is moreover well known to the police who keep the file of his crimes up to date: he has already raped then murdered (or, in some cases, murdered then raped) twelve girls between the ages of thirteen and fourteen since the beginning of the school year, and always by particularly horrible methods, of which the material details figure in the report with a good deal of objectivity and a wealth of specific detail. It would even be quite impossible for normal investigators to reconstruct in this way the series of brutalities suffered by the victims, given what little is generally left of their bodies, if the report were not supplied by the criminal himself. The procedure has, in fact, been judged to be more convenient for everyone, since in any case the man's identity was clearly established, with his names, nicknames, given names, various addresses, acknowledged professions, and schedule.

If he has not been arrested long since, tried and sentenced to death in the electric chair, it is because he belongs to the regular staff of the municipal information service: he is, specifically, the chief informant belonging to a terrorist organization, in which he holds the chair of sexual criminology of a kind of revolutionary night school. His favorite victims are, for this reason, the daughters of Wall Street bankers who are a little too reluctant to hand over their voluntary assessments, demanded each month by the group's treasurer. Statistics concerning the accidental mortality among girls of this age group show that such a tolerance in the functioning of the city police is ultimately much less mortal than deaths by drowning, camping in the Adirondacks, vacations in Europe, having to cross more than three streets to reach school, and ten other activities which it would be out of the question to forbid. The only mysterious point in the case remains the presence in the subway, at this hour, of children who are in principle very closely watched and who have at their disposal all the limousines, with or without chauffeurs, they could desire to get from place to place.

Thus the blond girl who has just been killed was the niece and sole heiress of an influential figure previously mentioned: the man who lives on Park Avenue, between Fifty-sixth and Fifty-seventh Streets, in an apartment decorated to look like that of an avant-garde millionaire. I have already told the story, to wit, of the lovely auburn-haired adventuress sent to him first as a lure, in order to effect the collection of his assessment by more humanitarian methods.

"You have just said that the adolescent girl had stepped onto the metal platform between the two cars, during the subway stop in the previous station. She was therefore, at the moment Ben-Saïd stood up, not being pursued by the sex fiend whose existence you are obviously making up on the spot . . ."

"Yes she was. She was being pursued and even worse, as I'll explain right now. But the boy in the black jacket, indicated by the letter W in the report, couldn't know that. He thought that the girl's violent gestures, at first made inside the next car, against the little pane of glass, then in the space separating the two cars, constituted indications she was giving him at a distance for carrying out his job. However, these arm and head movements were so rapid and confused that he could not manage to figure out what they meant. Actually, they consisted of a chaotic mixture of calls for help and desperate struggles against the aggressor. The boy had also not noticed, because of the distance and the two intervening panes of glass, as well as because of the very dim light in the area between the cars, that the girl's clothes were torn and covered with blood from the waist to the knees, and that there was also fresh blood spread all over her neck and her right hand."

"What had happened to the other boy during all this while?"

"What other boy?"

"The one indicated in the report by the letter M."

"M didn't go with them that night. He had stayed at home to watch an educational documentary about Equatorial Africa on television."

"You say that the victim screamed. Yet neither Ben-Saïd nor W heard any scream or any sound of a struggle."

"Of course they didn't! The racket of that old subway express train is much too loud, especially on the curves. But that whole part has been recorded on the tape heard by J. Robertson in the uncle's apartment, as I have already indicated."

"That tape, if my recollection serves, included no noise of wheels nor groaning metal, only the sounds of a struggle—material torn, panting breath, moans— and the great final scream when the victim was thrown out onto the track, left foot tied to a cord attached to the railing on the platform."

"It must have been because that tape was edited. Or else there was some special magnetic device which doesn't record sounds produced by metals."

"The first time, you mentioned, between the struggle and the final scream, moans of an altogether different nature, which you were glad to suggest referred to pleasure. How could a girl so young participate in that fashion in a particularly brutal violation and in knife wounds inflicted on her own body?"

"They weren't the victim's sighs, of course, but those of the murderer. And if you need any further proof in this matter, there are as usual the pieces of evidence gathered at the night's end by the transport workers: the large patches of blood on the floor and the walls of the car, the various filthy fragments, recovered under a bench, of the schoolgirl's black dress and white underwear, and finally the thin hemp cord whose origin is certainly the same (one of the three strands composing it is noticeably thicker than the other two in consequence of a systematic defect in the manufacture) as those the murderer has always used to tie up his victims in various ways before, during, or after the operation."

As for the murderer, he is none other than M himself, of course, as his initial indicates. He merely wore a hoodlum's mask over his own face. Laura suspected as much right away, luckily for her, alerted by the excessively composed voice of the pseudo-youth, which had permitted her to notice the ill-fitting edge of the plastic film, under the right ear. It was to examine this detail at closer range that she pretended to embrace the boy, as has been said. And to ridicule him, she murmured later on, as she ran away, "Don't forget to set fire to it, Mark-Anthony!"

The latter is now standing, then, behind the rectangular pane of glass at the end of the car whose little door he does not succeed in opening, since Laura has taken the precaution of removing the inside latch before seeking refuge on the connecting platform. He is, after all, she tells herself, too violent and too stupid. He came very close, this time, to hurting her seriously. She examines, turning it over so that she can see all sides, her right hand which is covered with blood: there is enough light to see that the wound is superficial. Then she ventures another look into the other car: the man in the yellow coat is sitting down again, now; he is watching W who has just stood up in his turn and is moving toward him, not with the determined expression of a delinquent boy who wants to terrorize a timid bourgeois, or of a person who happens to meet an old friend, or simply of the solitary passenger who has decided to join his sole traveling companion, but on the contrary with all kinds of halts, detours, and roundabout movements from one end of the car to the other, as though attracted by the huge panes of glass behind which pass, at a speed all the greater occasionally, the closer they are, the vaulted walls of the subway tunnel, blackish surfaces where the lights of the train reveal in passing the sudden recesses, the niches constructed here and there for possible pedestrians, the signs and figures lacking any apparent meaning which doubtless appear here for the exclusive use of the conductors or of conspirators, the three endless cables which run in festoons about a yard from the ground. Sometimes the boy, seized by a sudden impulse as though some sudden interest had summoned him elsewhere, abruptly abandons his hesitant manner and his vague expression to hurry a little farther ahead, that is, a little closer to Ben-Saïd. But this may be only the effect of an unexpected jerk of the car, which has caused him to miscalculate his equilibrium.

The train, meanwhile, has passed through several local stations without slowing down, revealing only an occasional passenger sprawling on a bench, waiting for the arrival of a bus connection. It now comes to a halt in a larger station, though one as little frequented. Ben-Saïd, who has recognized the name of the stop, "Johnson-Junction," quickly stands up in order to get off, walking over in front of the central doorway where he waits for the complete immobilization of the train and the automatic opening of the sliding doors. The young hoodlum is then very close to him, and comes still closer in order to be standing, himself, in the immediate proximity of the exit; but he turns his back, obliquely, as though to be inspecting the mechanism of the sliding doors, without seeming to be concerned with his neighbor.

Oddly, once the train has come to a stop, the doors of the car remain shut, whereas the characteristic noise of their normal functioning has been heard from one end of the train to the other, and already the passengers emerging from the neighboring cars are passing on the platform, in front of Ben-Saïd. The latter vainly tries to pull the brass handles apart. Then he runs to the other two doors, one after the other, without any more success: all three are jammed shut. On the platform, behind the first doorway, there is a man in a white coat who, trying to get into the car, also tries to work the outside handles. He exchanges gestures of helplessness with Ben-Saïd; then he says something—perhaps five or six words—but no sound passes through the thick glass, and at the same time the man points authoritatively at the central door, where the boy, for his part, shows no impatience. Before Ben-Saïd has been able to grasp the meaning of his technical advice, the passenger in the white coat, who has gray hair, gives up with a shrug of his shoulders and walks toward the next car toward the head of the train, its doors being wide open, in the normal position. He has just time to get in and immediately the dry click of the automatic closing echoes through the entire station, while the train moves ahead.

Ben-Saïd looks again at what the stranger in the doctor's coat seemed to be pointing at; he then notices that W is calmly withdrawing the blade of his knife which he had stuck into a slit in the safety mechanism to the upper left of the central door. It is the point of that knife blade which must have jammed the mechanism in the entire car, the boy carefully holding his knife by its ivory handle in order not to be electrocuted.

Ben-Saïd suddenly feels exhausted. He returns to the seat he was occupying at the beginning of the scene, at the front of the car. The boy, too, returns to his seat on the opposite bench, on the same side as the little door connecting the cars, and resumes his apparently unconscious toying with the brass latch, his shoulder letting it return to its closed position each time he shoves it upward.

Laura, who despairs of seeing the situation advance any further, since her clumsy accomplice pretends he does not even see the signals of impatience she has been making to him for the last quarter of an hour or even more, decides to intervene. She puts her hand on the brass latch . . . but just at this moment she sees behind the rectangular pane of glass above this, at the other end of the car, the very pale face of a gray-haired man in a dazzlingly white coat who stands motionless in the same way on the other connecting platform. He seems about sixty and is observing with surgical attentiveness the boy's hand resting, a couple of inches from him, on the inside latch. W cannot suspect that someone is spying on him in the darkness behind his back. As for Ben-Saïd, he keeps his eyes fixed on his knees.

The narrator has immediately identified the new character who has thus entered the scene, and whose pale face with its drawn features, thin lips, and penetrating yet tired eyes behind their steel-rimmed glasses now presses closer to the little rectangular pane, which also makes it possible to make out the five or six reddish-brown stains, the size of peas, which distinctly speckle the lapel of the coat, as Doctor Morgan, who is returning to his underground office at the Forty-second Street station after having given the injection which has been described. But Ben-Saïd cannot recognize him, since he does not see him, keeping his eyes fixed on his knees, fixed on his knees, fixed . . . the whole steel carcass of the train begins to creak louder now, fixed on his . . .

Retake. Laura stares at her red-stained hand. The light which comes from the two adjoining cars is enough, on the narrow platform, to see that the wound is superficial. She therefore has managed, once more, to escape her pursuers. Tonight, too, she has seen through their disguises and their devices. She puts her hand on the ceramic knob, but suddenly freezes . . . There is blood, a trickle of thick, fresh, bright-red blood flowing under the white door, coming from inside the room. This forms a kind of tongue about an inch wide whose slightly bulging tip advances rather slowly but regularly across the tiles toward Laura's bare feet.

Making a sudden decision, the young woman completes her interrupted gesture and opens the door wide with a single gesture, a violent push which makes the entire door vibrate, as it flies open, for a long time. Her white hand remains suspended in mid-air, in the open doorway, so great is her emotion before the spectacle presented to her widened eyes.

Inside the car, nothing has changed: Ben-Saïd's eyes are still on the floor, while W continues his regular, mechanical toying with the brass latch of the door, which breaks the silence with its too-loud and too-slow beat of some inordinate metronome. For reasons which have not yet been explained to the passengers—a breakdown of the current, sabotage, a light signal jammed by terrorists, a fire in the conductor's cab, a young girl's body lying across the tracks—

the train is immobilized in a tunnel between two stations for a period of time it would be difficult to determine. Laura, who is still on the platform connecting the two cars, listens, ears cocked, for some decisive occurrence: crackling of flames, bursts of machine-gun fire, alarm sirens, clamors of the revolution, or else the muffled roar appearing out of the distance and growing ever louder until it turns into a very close din of the next train traveling at full speed, since the track is free according to the jammed signal lights, and which bears down on the obstacle, invisible until the last moment because of the curve of the tunnel and which will therefore in a few seconds collide with the paralyzed train in an enormous explosion of machines shattering to bits, cars telescoped together, women screaming, windowpanes pulverized, steel twisted, benches torn out and thrown in all directions.

But on the roadbed, beside her, vague although very close, almost within reach of her hand, no doubt the attentive girl perceives only a faint wheezing sound, a short and scarcely perceptible breath . . . A dim, oblong, hunched shape is creeping along the rail which gleams faintly in the darkness. The thing soon reaches the brighter and more open space between the two cars, and Laura, frozen with horror, recognizes a rather large gray rat which, having stopped to stare at her with its tiny black eyes, raises in her direction a paler snout with sharp teeth at the sides, apparently trying to detect, in tiny, swift, slightly hissing sniffs, the odor of the raw flesh it is selecting in advance, waiting for the imminent catastrophe whose premonitory emanations it has already picked up.

In order to tear herself away from the fascination which risks making her step over the railing, if the halt continues, the young woman clings to the ceramic knob, which turns in her hand, and opens the door in a single, forceful gesture: the rat is there, creeping along the white tiles of the room, its claws producing a disagreeable crunching sound around the bloody body of the murdered girl. So she had not been mistaken when she had thought she detected the presence of a rat close beside her, the night she had been shut up without any light in the empty library on the ground floor, last night probably.

She had been so frightened that she had sought refuge at the very top of the empty bookshelves, climbing from one to the next, which had allowed her to discover, groping in the darkness, on the top shelf, the detective story with the torn cover she had afterward, in order to read it on the sly, carefully stored under a removable floorboard in her room, in that secret cavity where the gaudy volume had joined the box of matches pilfered from her guardian's pocket, one evening when he had entered her room in order to rape her and had then fallen asleep, exhausted by a long day of difficult assignments, shadowing people all over the city, and also the pair of sharp-pointed scissors he had brought her as a present from one of his nocturnal expeditions, in order to make cutouts, and which she pretended to have lost, the shiny steel knitting-needle discovered at the back of a night-table drawer, in a crack between the bottom and the side and extracted with great difficulty and then carefully sharpened on the tiles of the corridor, and finally the three splinters of crescent-shaped glass that looked like Arabian daggers, still stained with her own blood ever since the day she had cut her hand deeply while detaching them from the broken pane of the French window overlooking the fire escape on the top floor of her prison.

Thus this prison includes rats, like all prisons, which explains the tiny scratching, running, or creeping noises to be heard sometimes in the uninhabited regions of the huge building. And the captive had also not been mistaken when she thought she had heard, just now, more violent noises and long screams of pain coming from this room. The end of the sacrifice, as a matter of fact, can only have occurred a few minutes ago: the body seems still warm under the harsh light of the spotlights which are still on; in the middle of her outspread blond curls, the doll's face with its wide-open blue eyes and parted lips has kept its pink china coloring. And this face, without any possible doubt, is that of Claudia, the young friend of the day before who spent the afternoon at the house, who took tea with Laura and who played games with her, cutting out black paper masks.

After having sniffed the still-liquid blood, several trickles of which, varying in length, have run across the tiles, and glanced in all directions, the rat now grows bolder: it sits up on its hind legs and hesitantly moves its forelegs and its snout over the body of the victim lying on her back in an abandoned, limp position, her charms proffered rather than concealed by the torn and bloodstained shreds of the long white nightgown. The animal, which seems particularly attracted by the wounds of the seven daggers thrust into the tender flesh at the top of the thighs and the lower part of the belly, all around the sticky pubic hair, the hairy animal is so large that, while still keeping its hind legs on the floor, it nonetheless manages to explore the fragile lacerated skin from the anus to the area around the navel where the bare flesh reappears, still intact here, in a broad, fraying rip of the thin linen material. It is here that the rat decides to sink its teeth, and begins devouring the belly.

It seems as if a shudder has run through the victim's body, which is perhaps still alive, and that her mouth has opened a little wider. In order to try and escape this nightmare, Laura gropes in the narrow pocket of her dress, without being able to tear her eyes away from the spectacle. With some difficulty she takes out a tiny pharmaceutical capsule which she unhesitatingly swallows.

Retake. Laura does not understand why . . . The long naked legs, one of which is half bent at the anus and at the knee . . . No! . . . The ankles are now spread wide apart by hemp cords which encircle each of them several times and fasten them separately to the heavy cast-iron feet of the two spotlights; but one of the cords is twisted, where the leg is slightly bent. No! . . . Under the bright light of the other two spotlights, another rip in the nightgown, which runs from the neckline to the armpit, reveals a very long neck, the smooth, rounded shoulder, and most of a full breast whose aureole seems rouged with sepia. A cord also encircles the arm, three loops sinking deep into the flesh and pulling back the elbow, doubtless toward the other one; but the other elbow is not visible, nor are the wrists and hands, hidden behind the back, probably tied together and fastened to the floor by some means. It is clear that the way in which the girl has been fettered has permitted her to twist her body and to struggle, but within calculated limits, only for pleasure's sake. On the floor, about a foot and a half from the bare shoulder, is a half-smoked cigarette from which the smoke is still rising in the calm air, in a thin, . . . This time the body has moved, no doubt about it: the head has rolled on one side, the bent knee bends still farther, which has tightened the cord. The rat . . . No! No! Retake.

Laura does not understand why the train has halted this way, right in the middle of a tunnel, with a long screech of brakes and clashing metal. In the sudden silence, she glances right and left at the two little connecting doors. But there is only one possible way out, since in the car she has just left The Subway Vampire is still there, behind the glass, trying to work the latch in order to catch up with his prey, fortunately with no success.

She has managed, then, once again, to escape her pursuers. She has, tonight, too, seen through their disguises and their devices. She brings her left hand to the brass handle which will give access to the other car, but immediately freezes: at the other end of the car, behind the symmetrical pane of glass, Doctor Morgan, the sinister criminal surgeon, has just appeared, with that motionless whitish face he always has in the newspapers, but which must be a mask. His thin lips, his drawn features, his penetrating yet tired eyes behind the steel-rimmed glasses are there, quite recognizable, pressed against the pane, watching the victim specified by the orders of the day, around whom the network closes in . . .

This second escape cut off in its turn, Laura lets go of the brass handle and prepares to step over the metal railing, in order to run away along the tracks, taking advantage of the fact that the train is still, miraculously, halted. As she peers in the darkness of the roadbed for the best place in which to jump down, she then meets the gleaming black eyes of a huge, motionless, threatening rat, one of those countless repellent and dangerous animals with which the tunnels are infested, as is natural since the tunnels communicate with the sewers. The animal from the depths seems to be waiting for her to eat her up alive, or in any case to maim her, to disfigure her, to give her the plague, cholera, exanthematic typhus . . .

With an instinctive gesture, Laura hurls into the animal's face the brass handle she has kept in her right hand, after having pulled it out of its fastening at the other door, when she was making her escape. She has just forgotten, in her hysteria, that she had decided to keep it as a weapon in order to strike her aggressor, if he caught up with her, with something more dangerous than her tender fists. The gesture moreover was quite useless: the rat leaped into the air, all four feet at once, to avoid the clumsily aimed projectile, and landed exactly where it had been without having been touched, now spitting out its poisoned breath at the henceforth defenseless enemy, to make her understand its own determination. The girl sees in a flash that the net has now closed over her. She gazes in despair at the piece of solid, pointed metal she has just thrown away so foolishly, whereas she was hoping, even a few seconds before, to carry it back to her room in order to hide it with her other weapons under the removable piece of flooring.

Laura has no time to puzzle over the possible means still remaining available to her, nor over the fate which will meet her in case of failure. Before she has been able to discover the least piece of metal to detach from the jointed structure constituting the narrow

platform and its railing, the two little doors have
opened at the same time and two men have taken
hold of her, each one grasping, with vigor and exactitude, one of her wrists, on the left side Doctor
Morgan, whose massive figure has passed through the
entire car without her having either heard or seen
anything, and on the right, M, The Vampire, who has
finally managed to work the latch open with the help
of a pair of pointed scissors which happened to be in
his pocket tonight (by accident?), as has already been
said.

The calm strength of the two men, who are thus
holding her in a double vise, renders any resistance
vain, affording something restful to the body as to the
mind—even something agreeable, in a sense. In less
time than it takes to write it (thinks Ben-Saïd, who
without leaving his seat has half-turned around to
watch the scene) the girl finds herself dragged to the
middle of the car, the central door of which has been
opened at the same moment by W, who has skillfully
inserted the blade of his knife into the safety mechanism (which he tested at the previous station, altering
its normal operation in accord with his personal decisions), and there forced to get down onto the tracks,
still framed by her two guardians who are squeezing
her wrists so tightly that already she can no longer
even feel her hands. There are only five or six steps to
take, on the narrow path alongside the roadbed, before all three vanish into a recess in the wall, its rectangular slightly-vaulted opening resembling the
usual shelters located at intervals along the tunnels.

At this very moment the car door has closed, and
the train has immediately resumed its course, interrupted by the conspirators without the mechanics

having suspected a thing. Leaving his position of command, W says "There we are!" and returns to his bench at the end of the car, rubbing his hands together two or three times. When he passes the false Ben-Saïd, he gives the shoulder of the shaggy coat a heavy thump of complicity, which makes its wearer start. Then W sits down opposite him, exclaiming for the sake of the petit-bourgeois homosexual from whom there is no longer any need to conceal the conspiracy: "Making out?"

Ben-Saïd, who is describing the scene with laborious care in the notebook with worn imitation-leather covers which he had taken out of his yellow overcoat pocket at the moment the train came to a halt, in order not to waste time, utters a vague acquiescence and continues to cover his cross-ruled page, slowly but without erasure, with tiny careful letters whose regular alignment is virtually unaffected by the jolts of the moving train.

W continues: "Took care of that one!" Ben-Saïd acquiesces again by the same vague grunt and continues writing. He has reached the moment when Laura, still firmly held by the two giants who are twisting her arms backward slightly in order to prevent her from initiating any resistance whatever, is pushed ahead of them into that corridor whose entranceway resembles the shelters for linemen, but which gives access, after a completely dark and winding, long, passageway, to a cubical chamber dimly lit by a bare bulb dangling from a wire. The ground, the four walls and the ceiling are covered with that same once-white ceramic tile which is used everywhere in the subway stations and entrances and which is here in a somewhat better state of preservation. The only furniture is an unfinished wooden table and two un-matching chairs, both old and dirty, the kind to be found only in the wretched kitchens of the Southern states, reconstructed by television.

As soon as they arrive, M has closed the entrance to the corridor by pushing shut a heavy iron grille, then turning the key in the lock (the key was in the lock, but he then puts it in his pocket), while Morgan sits down at the table and opens the drawer, taking out a red cardboard file which he spreads out in front of him. A white sheet and a gold pen with a retractable tip, whose mechanism he operates carefully, as if it were a hypodermic syringe, complete his accessories. M will sit down on the other chair, which is a little farther away, against one wall. The girl, whom they have released once inside the room, as soon as the iron grille has been shut, has run away from them into a corner, as far as she can get from her two rav-ishers; here she crouches, huddled into as small a space as possible, as if she hoped to vanish into the walls, her arms encircling her knees. She has immedi-ately seen that there is no couch on which to rape her, which disturbs her even more. All there is in the room, besides the table and chairs, is an iron cage like the kind used for wild animals, about five feet square, whose bars, some six inches apart, are identical with the ones on the grille, which is to say, spaced so that not even a child could slip between them.

Doctor Morgan, who has completed his prepara-tions, utters a kind of faint, continuous, virtually un-modulated whistling. At this moment, a large gray rat —perhaps the same one as a moment ago—emerges from the darkness and creeps forward to the grille, thrusting only its head into the room, between two vertical bars. No one moves, but Laura keeps her eyes fixed on the animal, while the two men appear to be paying no attention to it.

A new whistling breath from the doctor, to a somewhat accelerated rhythm, and the rat jumps over the lower horizontal bar and enters the room; it continues creeping forward toward Laura, until it reaches the middle of the room, then comes to a halt, the whistling having ceased. Obviously the animal is obeying the surgeon, who is watching the young captive's reactions, squinting his tired eyes behind his oval lenses, and who any second now will give the signal to the animal to leap upon her. Laura is already calculating how it will spring, but a series of lower, and slower, notes changes the rat's orders, making it beat a retreat and vanish the way it had come through the corridor grille. Morgan takes off his glasses with his left hand and, with the bent forefinger of his right hand he rubs both eyes for a long while, one after the other. Then he places the glasses in the left outer breast pocket of his coat, takes from the outer right pocket a second pair which, from a distance, seem identical to the first, opens the red file and, while pretending to be examining several items inside, addresses himself to his captive without taking the trouble to look at her.

"So," he says slowly, in a tired voice, "you have understood. If you do not answer the interrogation properly, you will be eaten alive by this rat and several of its brothers, in tiny mouthfuls, beginning with the tenderest areas and running no risk of inflicting a quick death. This will take, of course, several hours. If, on the contrary, you answer all the questions as you should, you will merely be tied across the tracks just before an express train comes through, and in that way you will have no time to suffer. The choice is yours."

Then, after a silence, broken only occasionally by the sound of the papers he is glancing through, he continues:

"Let's see, your name is Laura Goldstücker, you are the daughter of Emmanuel Goldstücker who . . ."

"No, not the daughter: the niece," Laura says.

"The daughter," Morgan says, "it's written here on the first page of the file. Don't start twisting the words."

"The niece," Laura says. "My father was killed in Cambodia, during the thirty-day war. It must say so there, somewhere, in the report."

Morgan, who seems irritated, has bent over the table and consulted various typed and manuscript documents. He finally straightens up, holding in one hand a rectangle of heavy yellow paper, a kind of printed form which he waves in front of himself like a criminal lawyer: "Here we are!" he thunders. "Your uncle adopted you the following year."

"No," Laura says, "I refused."

"You were five years old," the doctor says, "how could you have refused? It was impossible, and you're impeding the interrogation. If we get into details of this kind, we'll never finish. So I repeat: you are the (adopted) daughter of Emmanuel Goldstücker, known as MAG, president of Johnson Limited, who is two months late in his assessments. For this reason, you have been sentenced to death this very morning."

"All right," Laura says, "is it a ransom you want? How much?"

"You fail to understand me: I said that you have

been sentenced to death. Such sentences are without appeal. Tomorrow, a little souvenir of your existence will be sent to your uncle-father, and our cashier will visit his residence that very evening. If he does not pay then and there, this time, his pretty red-haired whore, Joan Robeson, will be eliminated, but by means of much more complicated and cruel tortures which our clerk, Ben-Saïd, is at this very moment drawing up the list, in order to add it to the bailiff's summons. If that doesn't convince MAG, this document will serve in any case, on the following day, for the torture."

"What!" Laura exclaims, outraged. "They begin with me, and keep that whore in reserve! Just what I thought: the old idiot cares more about her than me. All I count for is to find out how serious your threats are concerning that precious little doll of his . . . But that's not how it's going to work out!"

"Yes it is," the surgeon says. "According to the report, that's just how it's going to work out. Moreover, it's quite likely that old Goldstücker cares more about his young mistress than about a child like you, who has never given him anything but trouble, though that is hardly the only motive which has led us to take action in this matter. Joan, as has been said, belongs to our organization; we therefore prefer to sacrifice her only as a last resort, after having tried every other means of recovering the money."

"But if she belongs to your organization," Laura says, "she actually runs no risk whatever."

"Quite the contrary," the surgeon says, "just think a minute: if we seem to be controlling her, Goldstücker will suspect something; and nothing in the world must permit him to discover the role she's been playing there for almost six months now. She must then, if that is how matters turn out, suffer the hideous fate Ben-Saïd is preparing for her. Since he is secretly in love with her, the program will doubtless be quite an interesting one."

"But what proof will there be?"

"There will be the report. You're forgetting that everything is set down there quite exactly, and that no tampering with the truth is permitted."

"All of which will leave a lot of deaths on your conscience," Laura says without much hope of convincing her executioner by such insipid arguments.

"Crime is indispensable to the revolution," the doctor recites. "Rape, murder, arson are the three metaphoric acts which will free the blacks, the impoverished proletariat, and the intellectual workers from their slavery, and at the same time the bourgeoisie from its sexual complexes."

"The bourgeoisie will be freed, too?"

"Naturally. And by avoiding all mass killings, so that the number of deaths (which for the most part, moreover, will be inflicted upon the female sex, always more numerous)—the number of deaths will seem quite low with regard to the work done."

"But why the tortures?"

"For four main reasons. First, it is a more convincing way of obtaining large sums from the humanist bankers. Second, the future society must have its martyrs. What would Christianity have done without Saint Agatha or Saint Blandine and the lovely illustrations of their torments? Third, there are the films, from which we also derive important revenue, quite out of proportion to the investments in spotlight lenses, cameras, color film, and sound equipment. For-

eign television pays very well for good productions
. . . For example, if we turn you over to the rats, as
the sentence provides, and the shots are properly set
up from beginning to end, with close-ups of the details and expressive cuts to your face, we have a German buyer who is willing to spend two hundred thousand dollars! In order to obtain their final agreement,
we have had to give them first a complete scenario as
well as a dozen photographs of you, six of which will
be stark naked from different angles, which have
necessitated the secret installation of several automatic cameras in your bathroom."

"Is it for an erotic program?"

"No, not necessarily. There is also the series of 'Educational Individual Crimes' which tries to effect a
general catharsis of the unacknowledged desires of
contemporary society. Do you understand the word
'catharsis'?"

"Certainly! Do you think I'm an idiot?"

"Sorry . . . And then there are also the films kept in
reserve for later, by speculators in the bull market of
history. You can imagine the value represented, for
any university offering the doctorate in historical
sciences, by optico-aural recordings of the execution of
Robespierre, Joan of Arc, or even Abraham Lincoln,
though much less spectacular than most of our productions."

Laura, who had, in fact, noticed the poorly concealed cameras in the walls of her private apartments,
especially in the bedroom, the dressing room and the
bathroom, but who supposed at the time that she was
dealing with a mere voyeur, her uncle for instance,
had done her best for eight days to assume, facing the
cameras, the most suggestive poses and expressions.

She now regrets having been so obliging. It is always a mistake to try and do a favor for people without making them pay for it. She says, in order to gain a little more time:

"You referred to four reasons. But you've only mentioned three."

"Well, of course, there is the pleasure, too, which we mustn't overlook either . . . But all this talking isn't getting us on with the job. I'd like to send you out to the drugstore to buy me a rare roast-beef sandwich and a cocaine cocktail. Only I'm afraid you'd lose your way in the dark corridors and then I'd never see you again. So let's get on with it: How old are you?"

"Thirteen and a half . . . But one last word: if I answer all your questions, what will your buyer for German television say? Don't you run the risk of a suit for breach of contract?"

"How naive you are!" the doctor exclaims, with a hearty laugh. "I can always decide that you haven't answered correctly. I'm the only judge. And in any case, there are questions which are so curious that I strongly doubt your discovering a suitable answer to them; not to mention the fact that the list of questions is never closed for good . . . All right . . . the capital of Maryland . . . how many seconds in a day . . . what do girls dream of . . . what do the windows overlook . . . you have already answered all that . . . Ah, here's something else: where did you first meet young W?"

"At the beach, this summer."

"When did you decide on this business with Ben-Saïd?"

"The man in the yellow overcoat?"

"Yes, of course—don't play dumb."

"Right then, when we saw him get into the car. At least that's what I thought, since he was actually in on it, you say. In any case, we'd been working on that line since the beginning of the week, and he wasn't the first one we'd taken to the last stop."

"What went on there?"

"Oh, nothing much: we had some fun scaring them and we took their money to buy tapes."

"Untouched?"

The child gave a shrill, unconvincing schoolgirl's laugh, then controlled herself at once: "No, it's no advantage to have them untouched, as you call it. For the same price you can get them with things recorded on them that you can always erase, if you don't like it."

"What kind of things do you look for?"

"Exciting things."

"Be more specific."

"Groans, sighs, muffled screams, things like that . . . Or steps climbing up an iron staircase, a pane of glass being broken, an iron latch creaking, and heavy footsteps coming closer down the corridor toward my room, whose door turns slowly on its hinges while I hide my face in the sheets. And then I feel the weight of the body coming down on top of me . . . That's the moment I start screaming. 'Keep still, you little fool,' he whispers, 'or I'll really hurt you,' and so on."

"You have used the word 'retake' two or three times in your narrative. What is its precise role?"

"The word all by itself?"

"Yes, between periods, whereas your sentences are for the most part correctly constructed, though sometimes a little loose."

"It seems quite clear to me. It means you continue something that had been interrupted for some reason . . . But you don't need to compliment me on my grammar—I'll talk."

"What kind of reason?"

"The reason, you old phony, that you can't tell everything at the same time, so that there always comes a moment when a story breaks in half, turns back or jumps ahead, or begins splitting up; then you say 'retake' so that people can tell where they are."

"Don't get upset," the doctor says in a low voice, sounding even more exhausted. "I understood. But you had to say it, so that it can appear in the report."

"Why bother?"

"Don't imagine that this report is made to be read by just linguists. Where were we?"

"The rape scene."

"Oh yes . . . Why do you need to steal a few dollars to buy these tapes, when you have all the money you want at home?"

"Money from the family isn't real money. It's fresh and smooth and has no smell, except the smell of printer's ink. The bills are brand new, as if they'd printed them themselves. The money you earn is all wrinkled, with little tears in it, and a little thickened by dirt; it feels good to the touch, and it has a good smell when you take it out of your pocket and put it down on the counter of a pornographic bookstore in Times Square."

"But you don't earn it, you steal it!"

"Stealing is a kind of earning, so is begging, or carrying dope, or doing things with nasty old men. It's all with the same money, the real kind, the money that's been used, that's dirty and smells good, like Havana cigars, French perfume, race horses, old cigarette lighters, and underwear before you wash it."

"No personal digressions, please. Go on with the story of what happens at the last subway stop."

"We get off, as usual, W holding hands with Ben-Saïd, who thinks he's stumbled over a safe little piece of trade he'll give five dollars to for spending a queer half-hour with him in some out of the way place. M and I follow about twenty yards behind, to keep an eye on things. I remember that in the station corridors, there was the big poster for the new Johnson detergent."

"The one of the girl covered with her own blood, in the middle of the rug in a modern living room furnished in white vinyl?"

"Yes, that's the one. Should I describe the arrangement of the body? The knives, the cords, and all the rest?"

"No, you've already done that about ten times. Just the text."

"The text says: 'Yesterday, it was a tragedy . . . Today, a pinch of Johnson enzymic detergent and your carpet comes out like new.' Above it, someone had written with a felt marker: 'And tomorrow the revolution.' When we got up into the open air, it was almost dark already. Ben-Saïd made no trouble about going to the empty lot."

"Which empty lot?"

"The one we decided on, when we put all that jumble in order, or tried to. Things haven't changed much since the last time . . . Now I suppose I have to give an exact description of the premises?"

"Of course."

"It's a kind of rectangular field about twenty yards by thirty, with very high fences around it, the only reason they're there is to put up big posters on them, there's nothing valuable inside. Only one door lets you in, a very little one, so low that you have to bend down to get in, and it's hard to find if you don't know about it ahead of time, because it corresponds exactly to the fake door shown on a photographic poster I will discuss a little later, if I have time. This is a plastic-coated advertisement made to resist the weather for several months, and that's been there as long as I can remember. Since it doesn't seem likely that it was pasted by accident in such an exact place, or even that anyone managed to adjust it over a previous opening, we must assume that someone (M, maybe, I've never trusted him, or else, why not Ben-Saïd?) has made the opening in the boards with a jigsaw, after the poster was put up. In any case, people don't imagine that a door printed on paper can actually open, and at the same time it's convenient for the ones who do know, it makes it easy for them to find it without difficulty, even when you've taken too strong a dose."

Inside there's very little vegetation: the ground is paved, the way the streets used to be, apparently. It seems like you're in a courtyard or a little square of some ancient town which was in this neighborhood and which has disappeared. Moreover the whole neighborhood is in ruins, for miles, but these are, actually, the ruins of rather recent houses, which were just badly constructed. Most of them are still inhabited. The little secret door has a key, which looks like a key to a real door. I'm the one who keeps it, since I'm the one who found it . . . No, I don't hide it under a removable floor board in my room; I always set it down, when I come in, on the marble table top, in the vestibule, beside the brass candlestick and the unopened envelope which is addressed to no one in the house, stuck by mistake in the mail slot, and which I should have given back to the postman I don't know how long ago.

But I'm coming back to this empty lot: it's strewn with discarded objects, arranged as I shall describe later on, among the tall weeds that have sprouted here and there in the cracks of the paving stones. Some of this debris is so big that it could only have been left here before the fence was built, for instance, the big brass double bed, with its metal springs and a ripped mattress spilling out tufts of rotting horsehair. And there's also a white Buick, a recent model in quite good condition, aside from the fact that it has neither wheels nor engine, and finally—and especially —a three-story iron staircase standing up in one of the corners, one of those skeletal fire escapes that city houses had at the beginning of the century, to save the inhabitants in case of fire. Now that I think of it, the bed could have been taken apart to get it through the little door, and then put back together inside. As for the giant staircase, it must have taken a huge truck and a crane, in any case, to get it here all in one piece; so it too could have been unloaded over the top of the fence. And the same crane could have taken care of the car too, which—door or no door—couldn't have been driven inside anyway, without wheels or engine.

With regard to the other objects abandoned in the vicinity, such problems do not come up. I list at random: a bicycle, a folding ironing-board, a jointed life-size female mannequin made out of pink plastic, still furnished with its auburn wig, doubtless coming from some department-store window, three movie cameras on cast-iron bases, a lot of television equipment, and a lot of other machinery even more nondescript and difficult to identify.

But I'm getting back to W who is just now reaching this neighborhood with Ben-Saïd; in the twilight, they walk past the big gaudy posters covering the fence. Just as the boy, having leaned against the secret door, looks up and down to make sure that the street is really deserted, a sound of running suddenly pulls him up sharp: several people, the quick footsteps echoing in the silence of this dead neighborhood, seem to be converging on this one place; and now a hysterical couple appears around the corner of the next block (the blocks here are the same size as everywhere else, but they are not blocks of buildings actually constructed: demolitions, abandoned foundations, sheds, blind walls constitute most of the landscape, where there are only a few one- or two-story houses standing).

W is careful not to reveal to these strangers, by some unguarded movement, the entrance to the empty lot, especially since other footsteps can be heard now, coming from the right and the left. He would prefer, moreover, not to be noticed himself; so he presses up against the big plastic-coated photograph without making a sound. Ben-Saïd, beside him, does the same. They watch the scene, which is suddenly lit up: the streetlamps have come on at the four corners of this block. This is probably the usual time, but for reasons unknown to the public, the ones at the other intersections remain unlighted.

Far from being reassured by this sudden illumination, the couple seems even more disoriented. It is a young man and a very young girl, both dressed elegantly, as if they were leaving the theater or a party. The girl is in a long, full, white dress, the boy in a black suit. Why are they walking in this wilderness? Has their car broken down? Or have they been kidnaped? They run a few more yards, but more uncertainly now, as if they were not sure of what was the best thing to do, the boy, a little ahead, trying to drag his companion with him, though she has turned around to look back. They do not speak a single word. Their faces are anxious; they feel they are being pursued, without even knowing from what direction the worst danger is coming. Soon they stand absolutely motionless.

The heavier footsteps of their pursuers have stopped too, close by no doubt, though no one appears anywhere. Standing in the middle of the street, the young people stare at the two intersections, one after the other, the one they came from and the one toward which they were running just now, being about halfway between them, which is to say, opposite the place where Ben-Saïd and W are hiding in the photographic image, as frozen as if they themselves were represented in it.

Then a man appears, at one of the corners, emerging from behind a shed which forms the end of the block; he takes three slow steps and comes to a standstill under the streetlamp, very easy to see. Another man appears in the same way immediately opposite, at the corner of the fence, to take up an identical position under the other streetlamp. And then at the two corners of the other intersection, two other men take up their positions. All four are wearing the same costume: a kind of grayish sweatshirt; they are bareheaded, with close-cropped blond hair; they are wearing black masks over the upper parts of their faces.

At each successive appearance, the young man has turned toward the new threat which has just arisen, guided by the sound of rubber soles, henceforth isolated in the great silence. Still very calmly, each of the four men takes out from under his sweater, where it was concealed by the loose material at the side of the chest, a heavy revolver which he immediately provides with a silencer, screwing on the device carefully, without hurrying. The weapon is made even more impressive by this thick cylinder which extends the barrel by at least two inches, when the marksman aims it toward the center of the scene.

The girl utters a scream of anguish, a single, hoarse, long drawn-out scream which echoes as in the closed space of a theater. In an impersonal voice, one of the four men (it would be difficult to tell which, for they are all exactly alike, and similarly arranged) tells the boy to walk ten feet toward the wall. His words are very distinct, each one pronounced quite separately from the rest, and the acoustics of the place are so good that he has no need to raise his voice, despite the distance. The boy obeys, under the threat of the four revolvers, after hesitating scarcely a second.

Then a kind of muffled explosion is heard, then another. The young man collapses and rolls across the pavement. Then there are two more explosions, and he stops moving altogether. At each shot, the impact of the bullet is distinctly perceptible on his body. The girl in the white organdy dress remains motionless and mute, as though paralyzed by fear in a slightly melodramatic posture: one hand half-extended toward her boy friend, the other raised to her lips, which open a little wider at each detonation. And she remains in that attitude, then, like a wax figure, her outspread fingers (one of them encircled by a slender gold ring) about six inches from her parted lips, her pretty blond head slightly turned away, her body leaning back, while the four murderers, with the same deliberation as before, unscrew the silencers from their revolvers and replace the weapons and the metal tubes under one arm.

Then they approach the girl, temporarily spared, and seize her without meeting any resistance. Nonetheless, for safety's sake, they gag her and tie her hands behind her back before they take her away, walking fast, supported, almost carried by two of her ravishers who hold her tightly by the arms on each side. At the intersection, they stop a moment: one of the two others leans down to pick up from the ground the long white veil their captive had lost, just now, in her flight, and delicately puts it back on her head. In a few quick strides, the group has vanished down the cross street.

All that is left on the asphalt, ten feet away from the dead man, is a little white circle which, on closer inspection, turns out to be a wreath of orange blossoms made out of plastic. When, at dawn, the police assigned to collecting corpses will find this body, they will also discover in the young man's hand a calling card or at least a piece of white cardboard in the shape of a calling card, with these words written on it in capital letters: "Young brides, in white raiment, will be torn, still virgin, from the arms of their earthly spouse, to become the prey of the knife and the flames . . ." and underneath: "Apocalypse, 8-90. Free Warning."

It is Ben-Saïd himself who tells us the story at "Old Joe's," where we are sitting around a table, as we do every evening, in front of our Bloody Marys. He put, he says, this random signature in the dead man's hand in order to take care of any eventuality. But now he wonders if it was such a good idea, for (he carefully checks the notebook accounting for his movements) it was not the hour indicated, nor even the exact place. He in any case is never late, he repeats bitterly; if he got there, this once, too close to the beginning of the scene, of which he might have missed a fragment, it was obviously because he had been given the wrong time, and perhaps on purpose, if someone is trying to put him in the wrong. Seven minutes' difference is a lot! And it was stipulated: "inside the vacant lot," which he had, for this very reason, already taken the trouble to describe. Or else it was an altogether different scene, and the men assigned to do the shooting belonged to an altogether different group. The whole thing, moreover, had seemed to him too neatly set up . . . "A mess!" he sighs. "The mess gets worse and worse, and I'm getting sick of it all."

But at this moment Frank arrived, walking through the door in that casual way, and sat down at our table as if he had heard nothing of the conversation. "Mission accomplished?" he asked. "Mission accomplished!" Ben-Saïd answered. And he has not made the slightest allusion to the minor discrepancies of time and place, nor to his dissatisfaction.

I went home immediately afterward, for Frank had —it seems to me—nothing to say to me. I took the subway, where everything seemed calm enough. The express car, which I got into at the stop where you change from the local, was empty, except for a very young girl in black leather slacks and jacket who, keeping her back toward me, kept staring through the pane of the little connecting door at the far end of the car. She reminded me of Laura, for some reason. I had the feeling, once again, that she wasn't happy. Opposite my house, the man was still at his post, in the recess of the wall. Without stopping to make conversation, for I was in a hurry to get to bed, I greeted him with a familiar "Hello!" He answered in the same way, as though in echo.

When I put my key into the lock, I had the momentary sensation that the mechanism had been tampered with: something unaccustomed was stuck inside, almost imperceptibly. Still, the key turned normally, and the door opened. I went in, closed the door behind me without making any noise, and put the key down on the table next to the unopened letter dropped in my box by mistake, which I should have returned to the postman I don't know how long ago. I once again made out the name and address, but it meant no more to me than the other times. On the back, there was still no mention of the sender. Again I had the impulse to open the envelope, then I decided that I wasn't so interested, after all.

I went up to the third floor and there I found Laura in her nightgown, her bed lamp in her hand, turned out, of course, the wire stretched across the floor, over the threshold of one of the empty rooms whose door was wide open, the room with white tiles.

I asked her what she had been doing there. She answered that she had been testing a plug. When I insisted on further explanations, and tried to find out why, furthermore, she had not gone to bed at this late hour, she led me to the center of the room and pointed at the two neat round holes which are set in the middle of one of the ceramic tiles. She had noticed, she said, that these holes were lined with brass.

"This must have been," I immediately answered, "a dining room, which explains the tiles. The plug was used for a bell, or a lamp in the center of the table, during the meals. Moreover, there is no indication of a chandelier in the ceiling, nor of any other kind of lighting in the room." But I had immediately sensed the danger: I already knew what she was getting at.

"The holes of a plug," she said, "are not threaded inside. Moreover, to make sure, I've just tested them: the diameter is too great, and the holes are too far apart."

"Then it was probably to screw something down."

"Yes, that's what I decided," she murmured, as though to herself.

I added, with the indifferent expression of someone who attaches no importance to such nonsense, especially after a long day of exhausting work:

"There are lots of odd installations in this house."

"Yes," she said.

"I've noticed many other incomprehensible details."

"Incomprehensible is not the word," she answered, after a moment's thought.

To change the subject, I said that she would catch cold, walking around barefoot on the tiles. That was when she told me about the man in the black raincoat who was watching the house.

I told her that she was talking nonsense, and I started to push her out of this room, where she had no business to be . . . Before I touched her, she had leaped out of my reach, taking refuge then in the corner farthest from the door. Here she crouched, huddled into as small a space as possible, as if she hoped to vanish into the walls, her arms encircling her knees, as has already been reported. I have also described how I slowly approached her, on the diagonal axis of the empty room, ready to make a quick swerve to the right or left if she attempted to escape me. But she made no movement, merely beginning to whimper like a dog on a leash.

I grabbed her by one wrist and pulled her to her feet. Then she began to struggle, but it was too late: she was imprisoned in my arms and her vain efforts to free herself had no effect except to make her weakness more apparent, while rubbing her body agreeably against mine, so that I continued this particular phase a few minutes longer, for pleasure's sake. Naturally I immediately desired her, and I dragged her toward her room, at the other end of the corridor, twisting one arm behind her, in order to give her a sharp pain if she should try to stop walking. But I stopped twice on the way in order to make her press up against me again and to make her suffer a little more, in that position, feeling against my rough clothes the tender friction of her belly and breasts through the delicate rumpled silk of her nightgown.

The door of her room had remained opened; the bed was already unmade. I pushed my captive inside and kicked the door shut behind us. Still holding her in the same way, I forced the girl to kneel on the white goatskin rug; without releasing her, I sat down facing her on the edge of the bed. Then I immobilized her wrists behind her back in one of my hands, and with the other, the right one, I slapped her several times, quite slowly, on the pretext of punishing her for not yet having gone to sleep.

Then I brought her head close to my face, taking a handful of her loose hair in my right fist, just above the nape of her neck, and I caressed her mouth with my lips. Since she did not seem to me to be sufficiently obliging, I slapped her again, without further explanation. After the third punishment, she kissed me without reticence, with all the care and sweetness I could require. Then I made her stretch out on her back across the bed, her fragile wrists still imprisoned together behind her back, in my left hand, and at the same time I pulled her nightgown up above her breasts; and I half lay down on that defenseless flesh.

For a long time I stroked her skin with the finger tips on my free hand, in all the places where the flesh is most delicate, but more to make her feel her helplessness than to interest my captive in my own intentions. Soon, under the threat of other, more barbarous tortures, I forced her to open her thighs, parting them with one of my knees, my wrist stuffing the delicate material down her throat as a gag to choke her a little with each application of pressure, as a means of additional persuasion. But from that moment, she abandoned any impulse of resistance, and obeyed my orders without question.

It was that night that I fell asleep beside her, all my clothes on, forgetting that there was a box of matches in the pocket of my coat, flung to the foot of the bed, which she could have reached by making a simple gesture without running any risk of disturbing my sleep. Yet it is the unconscious anxiety about those matches which immediately appears in my dream. I am walking down a deserted street, a street lost—I know it is lost—somewhere in a ruined suburb, in the bluish half-darkness of the early evening. There is no noise, not the faintest hum of traffic in the environs, and it is in a total silence that I hear myself saying: "Something gentle and desperate," which doubtless refers to this calm landscape, the tumble-down walls, the twilight.

The second sound which lacerates this tranquillity is that of the matches which I strike one after the other, trying to see the subject of the huge posters along a very high fence, which forms a smooth, impassable surface on my right. Without my knowing exactly why, it is very important that I make out the texts and images of these advertisements. But the faint, brief light from the tiny fugitive flames, which I must protect with one hand, does not manage to reveal anything in the shadows but certain details so enlarged by their immediate proximity that it is impossible to attribute any meaning to them, much less relate them to a whole.

Fortunately, streetlamps of an unusual power and height are now suddenly turned on, in every direction at once; and I need merely step back in order to look at the posters, which have nothing exceptional about

them, moreover: they are the ones to be seen everywhere, in the subway and other places. Among them is
the face, enlarged to the dimensions of a drive-in
movie screen, of a young woman with parted lips and
blindfolded eyes; the only remarkable (but not exceptional) detail of this particular one: a giant graffito,
painted with a single stroke of an airbrush, representing a male organ about ten feet high, raised vertically
to the parted lips. The poster thus disfigured, although recently put up, also includes five words added
to its own laconic text—"tomorrow . . ."—which is
completed by this manuscript judgment: "the ax and
the stake!"

There is also, right next to it, an electric iron the
size of a locomotive, all its chromium gleaming, as
complicated as a whole factory, and for a caption the
familiar slogan: "Warm as paradise, exact as hell,"
which is a phonetic allusion to the manufacturer's
brand name. A little farther on spreads the image of a
very smoky bar, of enormous proportions, where customers—all men—are sitting at tables in front of
glasses filled with the same red liquid, from which it
seems they are hesitant to drink; their severe, drawn
faces, as though in anticipation of an imminent event,
express moreover none of the sentiments one might
expect to see in praise of the warmth of an apéritif.

I recall the advertisement, also, of a large clothing
store which is offering special prices to young people
getting married: the photograph represents an elegant
young man in a black suit, accompanied by a blond
girl wearing the traditional gown of white organdy
with the transparent veil and the wreath of orange
blossoms. They are just over life-size, and run forward, holding hands. The pretty bride has her other

hand outstretched, as if she were trying to catch something; her lips part as though to speak. But no sound emerges from her mouth, and her gesture remains frozen in mid-air, her hand not closing over anything.

The next poster is also a very good reproduction of a color photograph. The subject itself is this time so widespread that its natural size has sufficed: it is the façade of my own house. I recognize it immediately by the three imitation-stone steps, the top one with a chip in the corner, and by the design of the cast-iron grille which protects the little rectangular windowpane. Two figures stand to the left of the steps, on the sidewalk glistening with rain. One is Ben-Saïd, the go-between who on Frank's orders is keeping an eye on any of Laura's comings and goings: it is easy to recognize him with his shiny black raincoat and his felt hat pulled down low over his eyes. He must have been caught unawares by the camera, without having dared to run away or protest, for fear of waking suspicions if he seemed to be afraid of any publicity revealing his appearance in this part of town. But what interests me more is the boy in faded jeans and a scuffed leather jacket standing next to him in the picture, for I have never noticed the presence of this person in my neighborhood. The letter W embroidered on his breast pocket should correspond to the owner's initial; but it is not certain, judging from the general look of the boy, that his possession of a piece of clothing implies his legal ownership of it.

As I come closer I discover that, if the two human figures are in fact life-size, the door on the contrary—on account of the perspective—is slightly smaller than the one through which I enter and leave my house every day. Yet (and I cannot say this really surprises me) my key has no difficulty entering the little black hole which corresponds to the orifice of my keyhole, it turns in it quite normally and opens the lock. The door opens, and I merely need bend down slightly in order to get through the wall.

One question comes up now: how was the ascent of the three steps effected: I cannot have climbed them, since they are a photographic illusion. And yet I don't have any memory of having had to step over a threshold of any such height . . . On the other side, moreover, there is neither table nor brass candlestick nor big mirror, but a rectangular empty lot, where a sparse vegetation has pushed into the very visible cracks which crisscross the entire surface of a regular pavement. The place must have been used to dump unwanted objects; now, curiously, such things are not heaped up here in disorder, but spread over the entire surface like the pieces in a chess game.

It is doubtless for this reason that I say the word "play"; yet the game in question might have, rather, the character of a theatrical performance, and then the play in question would actually be the entire representation. The fact of the matter is that the most striking of these objects is a magnificent brass bed in the center of the rectangle, its mattress slit as though by repeated knife thrusts, spilling out its synthetic horsehair stuffing scorched by the sun and sodden with the rain. A naked mannequin, made of some flesh-colored elastic substance, is lying on its back on the bed, limbs spread out in a St. Andrew's cross, a magnificent red wig framing its milky doll's face with huge staring green eyes. The genitals are also embellished with a hairy tuft imitating nature, but this pubic hair seems improvised with no more than a handful of reddish horsehair, ripped out of the mattress and summarily pasted onto the pubic triangle.

Around the bed are arranged three powerful spotlights, all turned on and aimed, one at the girl's feet, the other two at the right and left of her head, illuminating the naked body as harshly as for some surgical operation. I have no difficulty identifying this lovely auburn-haired creature as JR herself, who has just been sentenced as a final threat to conquer the fiscal tardiness of her old lover, Emmanuel Goldstücker, which has already been discussed. The polished steel table intended for domestic ironing, which has been used for the beginning of the torture reported previously, occupies, moreover, in the background, about a dozen squares of the chessboard (the granite paving stones are about six inches on a side). Symmetrically in relation to the axis of the bed rises a third kind of torture device: a lumberman's handsaw, a powerful blade about a foot wide and six feet long which, lying horizontally a yard from the ground between two wooden stakes thrust into the cracks between the stones (and therefore about eight squares apart), points its sharp teeth up toward the sky.

Most of the other pieces have been mentioned during the preceding. Let us review: the white car without wheels, the iron cage for carrying wild animals in the subway, the voyeur's bicycle, several archaic agricultural machines including a chaff-cutter, a plow with a single blade and three wooden harrows with cast-iron points, two doors painted bright blue still hung on their frames and turning on their hinges, and finally the iron fire escape standing in a corner of the vacant lot, like an observatory, making it possible to survey both the rectangle circumscribed by the fence and the streets surrounding it. At the top of the staircase has been installed a television antenna, linked to many sets scattered over the paving (of which each occupies some six squares), which thus reproduce a good number of times, the length of the rectangle, the same educational program. One of these sets and the African images it was transmitting figures, as has been seen, in the scenario of the first act. Let us point out in conclusion, strewing the more open places of the stage space, a ten-gallon can full of gasoline, a bunch of chains of the size used to restrain very big dogs, four cast-iron weights each one weighing forty pounds, furnished with a huge ring and an inscription in relief guaranteeing the exactitude of their mass, a pair of pliers, a hammer, blacksmith's nails, a heavy cylindrical wood-file with very deep notches, a green silk dress showing signs of burns, two syringes for intravenous injections, three blood-spattered nurses' uniforms, dressmaker's scissors, a steel T square, a crate containing six bottles of a bright red liquid, a depilatory tweezers, a notebook covered with black imitation leather, a felt-tipped pen, twelve razor blades, a knitting needle, pins, etc.

Without losing any time, I pass through one of the blue doors wide open on the void, in order to get, thirty squares farther on, four chains about a yard long, each one ending with a snap hook. I return to the bed by the same route; careful not to rouse her too soon from her fainting fit and without altering her posture, I carefully attach (with the help of the chains) the red-haired girl's wrists and ankles to the four brass columns which constitute the corner posts of the bed; I am going to get the can of gasoline, which obliges me to cover twenty-eight squares diagonally and to open the other blue door, which I close behind me on my way back; I sprinkle gas on the horsehair which substitutes for pubic hair on the chained mannequin, I return the can of gasoline to its position (opening and closing the door) and once again approach the bed; I find in my coat pocket, where I had thrust it when I entered the empty lot, the box of matches already mentioned; I turn off the three spotlights, strike one of the matches, and quickly brush it over the gasoline-soaked genitals, which immediately burst into flame.

A fine bright-red flame rises into the night, its swirls and spirals with their sudden bursts of color casting shifting reflections over the environing objects which seem thereby shaken with a tremor of their own, brief rotations and sudden starts, affecting in particular the closest bright surfaces, which is to say the open thighs, the hips and the chest of the young mannequin whose body and limbs contract under the effect of pain, but without her being able to make broader movements because of the fetters which pinion her so rigorously. Revived by this cruel method, the victim nonetheless pulls as hard as she can on her chains, producing a silvery clatter of barbaric bracelets, whose periodic spasms mark time to the roaring of the fire.

When the gasoline and the mossy pubic hair have finally burned up, the flame suddenly vanishes. I turn the spotlights back on. Lovely Joan now seems quite revived. Her eyes are wide open and gleaming, and she still fixes me with the same candid, amazed, unattached, rather childish gaze, and still has that same naively sensual smile on her parted lips, filled with promises, immutable and conventional both. The horsehair has vanished between her thighs, entirely consumed, and has left in its place a whitish, viscous substance which covers the pubic area with irregular trickles which I suppose are the remains of the glue, melted in the heat of the flames; I touch it cautiously with my forefinger which I then bring to the tip of my tongue: it has a pleasant taste, sweet and musky like that of certain tropical fruits. I tear another handful of horsehair out of a rent in the mattress; upon closer inspection it seems to me now that the vicissitudes of weather alone were not enough to have given it this fulvous color, which probably results from a dye, or from a red liquid which trickled out during the slitting of the mattress cover. While making these observations, I carefully arrange a thick and quite regular tuft which I apply, diligently following the shape of the corners, on the triangle of fresh-glued flesh, whose tip runs deep between the legs.

Then I repeat all of the previous operations: I go and get the can of gasoline and pour about a half-pint on the brand-new pubic hair of the young woman, who is as good as new all over again. I take back the can of gasoline, then I return to the bed where I turn off the three spotlights. I strike a match, taken out of the box which is in my pocket, and I set fire to the red tuft. This time the body with its voluptuous curves moves more, in the reddening explosions of the living torch, its bonds having doubtless grown a little loose, having been tugged in every direction by the girl twisting in a paroxysm of suffering. A kind of rattle emerges from her throat, with gasps and increasingly frequent screams, until the long final harsh moan which still continues after the total extinction of the flames, whose conclusion is marked by a shower of sparks. When I turn the spotlights on again, I discover that the wide-open green eyes are closed once more, and part only gradually now, in order to stare at me more intensely between the crushed-looking eyelids.

But I begin the ordeal all over again for the third time, as is called for in the text of the sentence provided by Ben-Saïd. And the victim stirs now, during the torture, most agreeably, while she utters words at random, a mixture of supplications and avowals, which come quite late as I take the liberty of reminding her. After the fire torture, I then move on, according to the program, to the torture with the saw and the pliers, which represents the third act.

Taking advantage of the exhausted state in which her last burns had left her (I had even stuffed a little horsehair inside the vagina in order to prolong the combustion), I detach the prisoner's chains from the bedposts, her gentle face with its imperturbable smile reflecting the joy of the young martyrs in the hands of their executioners. But without lingering too long over these metaphysical considerations, I tie her wrists together behind her back, tightly enough to keep them in the hollow of her hips and still leave the buttocks free. I take her henceforth docile body in my arms and place it astride the horizontal blade with the long sharp teeth, which is too high up for the patient's feet to reach the ground. I then chain each of her ankles to one of the forty-pound weights, which are placed symmetrically on either side of the saw, separated by an interval of five squares. The spreading of the long legs, stretched out by the chains, makes the steel points penetrate farther into the tender flesh of the perineum; trickles of blood begin running down the flat of the blade and the inside of the thighs, where the most abundant ones soon reach the knees.

In order to get on with the tearing-out of the toe-nails, then of the nipples, according to the regulation scenario recorded in the description, I must now go get the pliers, which raises a more delicate problem of routes than those I have previously had to solve. The torture device does not occupy, in relation to my own position, either one of the diagonal directions (the most favorable, since they permit me to cover a greater distance for the same number of squares), or one of the longitudinal directions, also permitted but less advantageous. I must therefore combine a fragment of longitudinal movement with an oblique (diagonal) fragment, this latter having to represent the greatest part of the route, so that the whole will permit me to cross the smallest number of squares possible. In order to select the best itinerary, I make various mental calculations, glancing over the squares, but I make several mistakes for the light is not adequate in all directions for the counting of the paving stones to be accurate, here in particular where the weeds are highest.

Finally I decide on a geometric route which seems likely . . . I realize, unfortunately, as I begin on my trajectory that I must have committed a serious error in my calculations; I correct it at the last moment, opting for a solution which is of course not the best one, but which I can nonetheless hope will solve my problem for me as well as can be expected. After a few squares, covered as usual by tiny strides of six or eight inches, being very careful about the interstices, on which the feet must never be set, I discover with alarm that I am farther than ever from my goal, whose exact situation I have great difficulty making out, moreover, amid the undergrowth, which now seems to me much higher than a moment ago. I advance in the direction which I imagine to be, more or less, the right one, and now all of a sudden I am cut off by the white Buick without wheels, whose low hood had remained hidden from view behind a thicket of brambles.

It is too late now to pretend to be on this route deliberately, so I must therefore stay at this point the time it takes to count to a thousand, so as not to have to pay the penalty corresponding to such a mistake. I have plenty of occasion, during this enumeration, to observe a very young couple in denim trousers and imitation-leather jackets, recognizable despite the similarity of these costumes, as a boy of fourteen (who has an inverted M on his breast pocket) and a slightly older girl (whose wide-open zipper down the front of her chest and all the way to her belly makes it easy to discern that she is wearing no undergarments whatever), who are kissing each other inside the car, sprawled on the comfortable cushions of the back seat.

Having discharged my obligation, I make a detour in order to continue on my route—what I imagine my route to be—which leads me on the contrary into a very dim area, where I soon come up against one of the blue doors . . . At least this is what I think when, hoping this time to get off cheaply, I open the door in order to walk through. The wooden door has already closed behind me, with a muffled click, when I realize my mistake: I am back in the middle of the wide empty street, in the bright bluish light from the streetlamps.

A few steps to my right is the old bald locksmith who is leaning over the image of my own door, trying to see what is inside through the little hole left by my key. He is doubtless trying to determine the cause of the piercing screams emanating from the interior and whose accents—unaccustomed, even in this neighborhood—have attracted his attention. And the spectacle which meets his eyes is certainly surprising: in the opening of a door painted bright blue located apparently at the end of some corridor, among undergrowth consisting chiefly of brambles and thistles, a young woman who is entirely naked appears in a three-quarters view, astride a sawblade with very sharp teeth, her legs pulled wide apart by chains attached to two rings, which hold her legs about eight inches above the stone-paved ground. The body's posture on the trestle (hands tied behind the back, hips arched, the auburn hair with golden highlights falling over one shoulder because of the tilt of her lovely doll's head) accentuates the exceptional beauty the tortured girl enjoys this evening: the slenderness of the neck, the waist, and the limbs, the resplendent plenitude of the flesh, the purity of the lines, the luster of the skin.

The victim, still shaken by charming contortions although already losing some of her strength, continues bleeding a little at the six points at which she has been tortured: the ends of both feet which seem to have been deliberately mutilated, the breasts whose milky globe is intact but veined by a whole network of red trickles which come from the gradually torn nipple and then flow down to the region of the hips and the navel, finally the genitals where the saw has penetrated deeper and deeper at each of the patient's convulsive movements, tormenting the flesh and severing the pubic region, smeared with sperm, much higher than the top of its natural orifice. (The girl seems to have been depilated beforehand, or shaved with a razor, or even singed by flame.) Blood has flowed in such abundance from this last wound that it has stained the anus and the belly, spattered the viscous, opaline substance with reddish streaks, with still shimmering layers covering the mound of Venus, covered the skin between the thighs and the knees, finally forming on the granite paving a little oblong pool surrounded by droplets. As for the sixth point mentioned just now, it is located in the rear and is therefore not perceptible from the point where the voyeur-locksmith is standing. This man notices, on the other hand, farther on, toward the far end of the room, a large brass bed with rumpled sheets.

The little man has set down his tool kit on the top level of the narrow doorstep. He has leaned his bicycle on the wall, to the left. I have already described how, having at last managed to see in some detail what was going on inside, this honest artisan hurried off to find help. Running off to the right, as Ben-Saïd has noted, he soon bumps into a harmless bypasser who is none other than N. G. Brown, the go-between assigned by Frank to watch the man in the black raincoat and the soft black hat with the turned-down brim, who meanwhile keeps watch under my own windows. Brown, who was walking more or less at random after leaving "Old Joe's," let himself be guided casually enough by his professional conscience; the latter has naturally drawn his steps toward West Greenwich. Since he had previously been at a masquerade party, for professional reasons of course, he is still wearing his tuxedo and dress shirt, as well as a fitted mask of delicate soot-colored leather, with only five apertures in it: a slit for the mouth, two small round orifices for the nostrils, and two larger oval holes for the eyes.

Without bothering with these details, which he scarcely notices because of his nearsightedness, reassured in any case by the man's height and powerful build, the locksmith leads him, while volubly repeating incoherent things, back to the house which he finds without difficulty, since his bicycle and his tool kit have remained in front of it. Here he quickly unlocks the door and opens the heavy imitation-oak panel with its old-fashioned hardware. He is then in the dim vestibule, cautiously hidden behind Brown who is beginning to suspect what the situation is. But the short bald man no longer sees anything, at the end of the corridor, of the disturbing scene he has just observed through the keyhole. It takes him quite a long time to understand that the surgeon in the white coat and the young unconscious patient lying in front of him, under the cone of harsh light, are actually located much farther away than he supposed at the time. His myopia often plays such tricks on him: it was in the mirror that he was watching the scene, which was occurring at the other end of the corridor, at the far end of the library whose door has remained open, as usual.

But now he is impeded by Brown's massive figure, for the latter has discovered at once where the action was, and his black, motionless silhouette fills almost the whole of the doorway. The short man is obliged to lean over still farther, in order to peer through the opening left between the jamb and the curving waist of the tuxedo jacket. A stranger to this story, he cannot identify Doctor Morgan, whom Brown on the contrary has recognized at first glance. Moreover the locksmith is more comfortable, given his position, contemplating the stripped body of the victim, her

amber skin, her fleshy pubic area, and the cruel operation she was being made to undergo, which I shall now
describe.

"Is there any need to? Don't you have a tendency
to insist too much, as I have already indicated, on the
erotic aspect of the scenes you report?"

"Everything depends on what you mean by 'too
much.' On the contrary, I myself consider that, matters being what they are, I have been quite restrained.
You will notice for example that I abstained from describing in detail the collective rape of the girl captured in the subway express by means of Ben-Saïd's
complicity, or the complicated tearing-off of the
nipples performed upon the Irish girl Joan Robertson, whereas I could readily organize, on each of these
capital events (which would doubtless have a considerable importance for what follows) several para-
graphs of enormous exactitude. I may add that I have
not even said what was done with the young bride,
nor described the torture—though extremely interesting, from a sexual point of view, because of the
imagination evidenced by the narrator on this occasion—of the twelve pretty communicants kidnaped at
the last moment from the real religious ceremony by
the fake Spanish priest. I would even have been
within my rights, it seems to me, to say at least how
they had all been crucified in different ways: the
youngest exposed from behind, head down, nailed by
the soles of her feet and the palms of her hands to a
Y-shaped stake, her charming and still intact buttocks
thus offered above the altar, after having had her
hairless genitals and her still unformed little
breasts . . ."

"I must stop you once again. You have several times

employed, in your narrative, expressions such as 'unformed little breasts,' 'charming buttocks,' 'cruel operation,' 'fleshy pubic area,' 'splendid red-haired creature,' 'luxuriant plenitude,' and once even 'voluptuous curves of the hips.' Don't you think you're exaggerating?"

"From what point of view would that be an exaggeration?"

"From the lexicological point of view."

"You regard such things as inexactitudes?"

"No, not at all!"

"Material errors?"

"That is not the question."

"Lies, then?"

"Still less!"

"In that case, I must say I do not see what it is you mean. I am making my report, that's all there is to it. The text is correct, nothing is left up to chance, you have to take it as it is given."

"No reason to get excited . . . One other thing: you mention West Greenwich or the Madison subway station—any American would say 'the West Village' or 'Madison Avenue.' "

"This time I must say you're the one who's exaggerating! Especially since no one has ever claimed that the narrative was being made by an American. Don't forget that it is always foreigners who prepare the revolution. Now where was I?"

"You had begun two stories at once, interrupted for no reason one after the other. On the one hand, the black mass in which you had sacrificed the twelve communicants, with the employment made that day of crosses, eucharists, candles, as well as huge candlesticks with iron points which serve to impale them. On the other hand, the way in which Sara, the lovely half-caste, had been impregnated by Dr. Morgan with sperm of the white race, extracted by Joan from old Goldstücker. Moreover, there is, in this regard, a contradiction in your narrative: you say in one place that the patient was naked, and in another that she was wearing a red dress."

"I see that you have not been following my explanations carefully: that was another day, another doctor, and another victim. The artificial insemination was performed not by Dr. Morgan but by a certain Doctor M. Moreover it is very difficult to distinguish them from each other because they are wearing the same mask, bought from the same manufacturer with the same purpose: to inspire confidence. This M's real name is something like Mahler or Müller; he runs a psychotherapeutical center in the Forty-second Street subway station. As for the girl in the red dress, that is not Sara, that is Laura; in that instance, the practitioner was not holding a catheter but a syringe for injecting serum—truth serum, of course. I nonetheless insisted on all these details, in their proper time and place. Dr. Morgan had been introduced into the narrator's house without breaking in, after having had a key made, quite simply, by a neighboring locksmith (and not like the psychotherapeutic family doctor, whom we shall call Müller, for the sake of simplicity, by breaking a windowpane at the top of the fire escape, according to what has been reported on several occasions).

"The day of the injection was also that of JR's execution; so Morgan was sure of finding Laura alone in the house (Ben-Saïd had carefully recorded the so-called brother's departure, and then his arrival at the empty lot). The purpose of the operation, easy enough to understand, was to find out, finally, who the girl is, where she comes from, and why she is hiding there."

"One last question before allowing you to continue: You have once or twice employed the word 'cut' in the body of the text; what does it mean?"

"An incision made by razor blade in the satiny, generally convex but sometimes concave surface of pink or white flesh."

"No, that's not it; I am talking about an isolated word, like the term 'retake' which we have already discussed, and concerning which you have, moreover, furnished satisfactory explanations."

"Then the answer is the same here (or, in any case, of the same order) as the one given on that occasion. It is a matter of indicating a cut in the course of a narrative: a sudden interruption necessitated by some material reason, purely internal or on the contrary external to the narrative; for example, in the present case: your untimely questions, which show the excessive importance you yourself accord to certain passages (even by reproaching me for them subsequently) and the lack of attention you pay to all the rest. But I shall continue, otherwise we shall never be finished. At the moment when N. G. Brown (often known as N, for simplicity's sake) bursts into the library, Sarah Goldstücker, the banker's real daughter (begotten long ago by the artificial means just described), is lying entirely naked, defenseless, heavy cords crisscrossing her body, except for her legs which Dr. Morgan has just freed from their fetters, in order to attach them forthwith in another manner, more in accord with his plans: the ankles and knees fastened tight to four rings attached to sixty-pound cast-iron weights, arranged more or less at the four corners of a square, which keeps the thighs wide open, their outer surfaces pressing on the stone floor and the knees bent at an angle of approximately forty-five degrees. The inner surface of the thighs, the anus, the vagina and above all the breasts are a somewhat paler hue than the rest of the flesh, dull and coppery, which reveals the mixture of white, African, and Indian blood, also betrayed by the mixture of indigo-blue eyes, inherited from her father, and the long, smooth, shiny and abundant hair, which is inky black with violet highlights."

The alluring face, the delicate and regular features, at least insofar as several strands of hair lying across the nose and cheek make it possible to judge (is the disorder of the hair the result of a struggle, or of careless treatment beforehand?), scattered curls whose spirals partly conceal the countenance, the disturbing effect being further increased by a red silk gag which distorts the mouth by sawing at the corners of the lips, not to mention the tilt of the head which the arms tied together behind her slant backward, the captive thus being unable to look in any direction except to the side, where, close to her left shoulder, her eyes wide with horror stare at the giant poisonous spider of the species called "black widow" which has just escaped from the surgeon, confused in his monstrous experiment, and has come to rest for the moment about six inches from the armpit, at the very edge of the circle of bright light cast on the floor by the powerful lamp with its jointed shaft whose base is screwed to the corner of the metal desk covered with papers, among which one white page as yet bears only brief manuscript notes, in the upper right corner, accompanied by an anatomical drawing of axial symmetry, the outlines precise and complicated, representing the vulva, the clitoris, the inner lips, and the entirety of the external female genitals.

But Doctor Morgan, who has eyes now only for the intruder whose identity he believes he divines under the mass, though still without being able to be certain, slowly stands up and begins retreating toward the other door. Since his rival hesitates as to what it would now be best to do, the surgeon takes advantage of this moment to regain the vestibule, step by step, his eyes still fixed on the slits in the black mask in which gleam two golden pupils; then, suddenly, he turns around toward the still wide-open door in order to leap down the three steps outside and—now pursued by Brown—escape as fast as he can down the straight street, running toward the subway entrance.

In the recess formed by the house opposite, Ben-Saïd, who was still holding his little notebook open and his pencil ready to write, notes the exact hour when he saw emerge one after the other, at three seconds' interval, the doctor with the steel-rimmed glasses who has not even taken time to remove his white coat, so eager does he seem to leave the premises (doubtless summoned by some appointment of extreme urgency), then the man in a tuxedo with the invisible face who has just entered the building with the help of the locksmith.

The locksmith has cautiously made his way down the corridor, after some delay, to the entrance of the house. And here, circumspectly holding the edge of the heavy door which he remains prepared to close at the first sign of danger, he sees the other two men vanishing on the horizon. It is at this moment that he hears a horrible scream from inside, unmistakably emanating where the captive is still lying. He whirls around and in a few steps again enters the library. In his haste, by an inconsistent reflex of cowardice, he has pushed the street door, which makes a muffled sound as it closes. Having again consulted his watch, the spy in the black raincoat and the soft hat notes the time on his memorandum.

The short bald man, realizing that he is now alone, closes the library door more calmly behind him, while staring, under the double cone of harsh light from the spotlights, at the young brown-skinned woman who is struggling hard in her bonds; and having come closer, he now understands what keeps her from raising her head or the upper part of her body: the cords which tie her torso and arms together, sinking deep into the flesh where it is tenderest and fastening the wrists up under the shoulder blades, are furthermore attached on the left and the right to the heavy cast-iron bases of the two spotlights. The unfortunate Sarah, who cannot beg for mercy or assistance, because of the gag lacerating her mouth, nor release her bruised hands, nor even move her shoulders, any more than she can close her thighs an inch, has seen the hairy animal, with which the doctor was preparing to continue his lunatic experiments, leap upon her, run zigzag over her bare flesh in tiny, rapid jerks broken by sudden halts, from the sweat-beaded armpit to the delicate neck, then toward the exposed belly and down to the hollow of the thighs, then back up the right side of the anus and the hip to the breast crushed by two rough cords which cross just under the nipple, finally over to the other breast, the left one, remaining somewhat freer between two twists of hemp whose proximity to one another nonetheless squeezes the delicate hemisphere, forcing the elastic tissue to bulge into a smooth, tight globe of pain, which seems ready to burst at the least prick. Yet it is this spot that the giant spider seems to have selected, wandering more slowly over these few square centimeters of hypersensitive skin, where its eight hairy legs produce the unendurable sensation of an endless electric discharge.

The locksmith voyeur, leaning over the scene because of his extreme shortsightedness, cannot tear his eyes away from this batlike body covered with a black fur with violet highlights, waving like tentacles an alarming number of long hooked appendices, if not from the harmonious lines of the victim exposed to its bites, rendered still more interesting by the fetters which bind her, squeeze her flesh, oblige her to remain in a cruel position, expose her utterly to the view of the onlookers. The most recent of these notices, in this regard, a curious detail: the equilateral triangle of fur, clearly outlined and of modest proportions, which embellishes the pubic area, has a splendid jet-black color like that of the animal itself.

The animal, having doubtless found, at last, the best place to bite its victim, has come to a halt at the edge of the swelling aureole, painted a bright sepia. Here, the chelicerae of the mouthparts, surrounded by continually moving maxillary palps, approach the coppery skin several times, then draw back as if they were licking or savoring in tiny mouthfuls a delicate food, finally attaching themselves to a point of the slightly grainy surface, speckled with lighter papillae, and slowly thrust in, pinching the flesh together, like the iron pliers with their sharp red-hot hooks, which are torturing another blessed virgin with the name of some iridescent stone, in a public square, in Catania.

The girl is then seized by violent, periodic spasms, producing a kind of shifting, rhythmical contraction which extends from the inner surface of her thighs to the navel, whose precise folds form, in intaglio, a miniature rose just beneath one of the excessively tight strands of the cord, which narrows the waist still more, making a deep curve above the hips and belly. Then the lovely head, the only part of her body she can move at all, flings itself convulsively to the right and the left, once, twice, three times, four, five, and finally falls back lifeless, while the whole body suddenly seems to go slack. Then, the girl remains motionless and slack, like one of those Japanese slave-dolls sold in the souvenir shops of Chinatown, abandoned to every whim, the mouth permanently silent, the eyes fixed.

The spider has loosened its jaws, withdrawn its venom fangs; its task completed, it climbs down to the floor, wavering slightly, makes another slow, broken line and suddenly, at a speed so great that it seems more like a shadow, leaps toward a corner of the room, climbs from shelf to shelf up the empty bookcases to the top, whence it had come, and where it once again disappears.

After a moment's thought, the short bald man extends a timid forefinger toward the coppery temple. The slender artery is no longer throbbing. The girl is certainly dead. Then, with gentle, meticulous gestures, he decides to set his toolbox down on the floor, having shifted it to his left shoulder after working the latch and kept it there since, during his comings and goings in the corridor. Then he kneels between the cast-iron weights, lies down carefully on the amber-colored body, whose still burning vagina he deflowers with a well-aimed thrust of the hips.

After some time, busy violating the warm and docile corpse, the short man straightens up, restores order to his clothes, runs his hands over his face, as if the upper part of his neck were itching. He scratches a long time on both sides; then, unable to stand it any longer, he pulls off the mask of the bald locksmith which covered his head and face, gradually ripping off the layer of plastic material and gradually revealing in its stead the features of the real Ben-Saïd.

But suddenly, just as he has completely removed the mask, whose limp skin is now hanging from his right hand, he wonders anxiously who it was that screamed, just now, when he was looking out at the street through the still-open door. It could not have been the dazzling half-caste terrorized by the spider, since the thick gag prevented any sound from passing her lips. Was there another woman in the house? Stricken with an irrational fear, Ben-Saïd opens the door to the vestibule and cocks his ears. Everything seems still in the huge building. He pushes the door farther open. Opposite him he sees his own face in the mirror, above the table. A little too quickly, without taking the requisite pains, he pastes on the conscientious artisan's mask again, checking his gestures as well as he can in the mirror; but the skin, poorly fitted, produces folds under the jawbone, and a kind of nervous tic twitches across the cheek several times, as though trying to put things back in place, to no avail of course.

There is no time to lose. At random, although no longer knowing exactly where he is and what he is doing, Ben-Saïd, by sheer force of habit, leaves a calling card between the bruised breasts of the corpse, after having written on it in clumsy capitals with his felt marker, using the marble table top as a desk, these words which seem to him appropriate to the situation: "So die the blue-eyed black girls the night of the Revolution." Glancing at an unopened letter which is lying there, he is once again seized by a series of tics running from the base of his ear to the corner of his lips.

Finally, having glanced around the entire scene, to make sure everything is in order, he replaces the leather strap of his tool kit on his shoulder. A last movement of his head toward the mirror, several still undecided steps to the windowpane where the over-complicated cast-iron pattern makes it difficult to see clearly what is outside, and he makes up his mind to face the street: with quick, abrupt little gestures, he works the inside latch, slides through the opening once it is wide enough, crosses the threshold, walks down the three steps, and walks away along the wall, taking hurried little steps until he is out of sight. It is only then, while the muffled click of the latch and the long vibration of the heavy oak door are still echoing in his ear, having been pulled shut by the doorknob in the shape of a hand, that the short bald man remembers having forgotten on the marble table top, between the brass candlestick and the envelope probably delivered in the morning mail, the skeleton key with which he had worked the latch and opened the door.

On the opposite sidewalk, in the recess of the wall, the man in the black raincoat and the soft felt hat pulled down over his eyes again pulls out his notebook from his pocket, takes off his leather gloves, glances at his watch, and writes down this event after all the rest.

Laura, meanwhile, who has heard the door slam shut, and observed through the window at the end of the corridor, at the top of the fire escape, the reassuring presence of her guardian, begins climbing down from floor to floor in order to inspect all the rooms one after the other, opening the doors one after the other, gently turning the ceramic knob, then pushing shut the door . . . This time she is certain she heard suspicious noises, but coming from the lower floors . . . It is, in fact, only at the last door, all the way downstairs, that she discovers the lifeless body of the young half-caste with whom she had been playing all afternoon . . . yesterday afternoon, probably . . . She approaches, without showing any surprise at the sight of the apparatus of cords, cast-iron weights and spotlights, to which her previous investigations have accustomed her, more astonished at seeing so little blood, even more astonished by the calling card whose text she reads over several times, without managing to grasp its meaning: "So die the blue-eyed black girls . . ."

The young girl, as a matter of fact, cannot guess the similar mistake made at the same moment by the false locksmith and a little earlier by Doctor Morgan. The latter, as has already been reported, has managed to make his way into the narrator's house at a time when he believes him to be detained far away by Joan's execution, she having been sentenced by the secret tribunal when her triple adherence to the Irish race, the Catholic religion, and the New York police was discovered. To get into the building is easy, thanks to the fire escape: it is enough to break a windowpane, thrust a hand inside, work the latch, etc.

The surgeon, guided by a kind of muffled moaning which comes from the lower floors, then climbs down the main staircase to the ground floor, where he discovers a young girl bound fast, which scarcely surprises him: this is doubtless the best way of keeping the little imprisoned ward from committing some foolishness or even from running away. As for the coppery color of her skin, entirely exposed, and as for the inky hair, they are also easily explained, although they scarcely correspond to the descriptions provided Frank by the spy on duty, describing N. G. Brown's secret companion on the contrary as blond, pale pink, and more or less pre-pubescent. This must doubtless be a disguise intended to deceive possible visitors, for Brown is not naïve enough to be unaware that he remains at the mercy of a check instituted, unknown to himself, by the organization. And in that case, isn't a dark skin the best guarantee of all? A black-girl's mask, a wig, the plastic film covering the whole of the body, including a few additional charms, is the sort of thing to be found in any store. The subterfuge is obvious, and betrayed immediately, moreover, by the captive's blue eyes.

Without proceeding to a more thorough search of the house, Morgan, who is convinced he is dealing with Laura herself, does not even take the trouble to check the artificial character of her epidermis. He is eager to pursue upon this new patient, before eliminating her according to his orders, the experiments he has begun some months ago concerning the poison of various tropical animals: yellow scorpion, black widow spider, tarantula, centipede, and horned viper. His intention—as is well known—is to perfect a vesicant product which, applied to certain specific regions of the external genitals of a woman, would be capable of setting off a series of increasingly powerful and prolonged sexual spasms, rapidly becoming extraordinarily painful, ending after several hours with the death of the subjects in the combined convulsions of the most intense pleasure and the most hideous suffering. Such a preparation would of course be in great demand during the great celebrations marking the triumph of the revolution, which must include, according to the program drawn up, in order to avoid a general massacre of the whites, a fair number of human sacrifices which would be particularly spectacular: collective rapes available to all passers-by on trestles set up at intersections and offering the city's loveliest creatures tied to special racks in various postures, theatrical performances in which certain chosen victims would be tortured in unheard-of ways, circus games revived from antiquity, public competitions for torture devices, tested before a jury of specialists, the most successful then being preserved—in the future society—as a legal means of execution, as was the case of the French guillotine, but in a much more refined class.

Unfortunately, Doctor Morgan has just lost at the same time one of his precious inmates (a fine white-ringed black widow from Mexico) and several of the most interesting pages of the memorandum he has been devoting to his researches. And now he is rushing like a madman through the endless corridors of the subway. And it is in pursuit of him that I myself am occupied. Yet I have long since lost all trace of him, and I continue walking, at a rapid, confident, regular gait, in the labyrinth of stairs and corridors, like someone who knows where he is going. Cut.

The trumpet player at "Old Joe's" then begins raising toward his lips the mouthpiece of his shiny brass instrument, suspended about six inches in mid-air beneath his brown lips still tense with the effort of a soloist in the middle of a fortissimo. In the huge smoky hall, all heads turn back toward him. Laura's hand, already curved around an imaginary sphere, takes hold of the white ceramic doorknob. On the tape, the scene resumes its course. Cut.

But I have been wondering for some time if Laura is not staying in this house on specific orders from Frank himself, who has assigned her the mission of keeping an eye on the narrator even in the most intimate hiding places of his own residence, even in his inadmissible gestures, his old habits, his secret thoughts. She is, in this espionage work, in constant liaison with the false Ben-Saïd, who is keeping watch on the sidewalk across the street. They signal each other through the windows. And from time to time, he slips her a book in code through the broken pane on the sixth floor, a book whose stains, tears, and missing pages represent the most important messages of their correspondence; which explains the state of my library, as well as the sudden appearance of new detective stories, as frequent and unforeseeable as their sudden disappearance. Cut.

The trumpet player at "Old Joe's" must be the same character, among others, as the man with the steel-gray face who has followed Brown to the fake psychotherapeutic clinic. Having heard, on the other side of the ground glass, the passwords exchanged by N with the nurse, he could easily have repeated them and thus managed to get himself into the heart of the story. Unfortunately, it is not known what became of him afterward. Cut.

I have also lost all trace of young Mark-Anthony, the boy wearing a stolen jacket with a letter embroidered over the breast pocket which might be the initial of the name "William." The leg of his trousers was torn on the occasion of the theft of the white car from a newlywed couple, a car which he must have later abandoned in an empty lot. Cut.

In pursuit of the criminal surgeon in the labyrinth of the subway shops under the Spanish district of Brooklyn, I once again pass in front of the big store dealing in religious items, which offers its customers imaginative clothes for communicants. In the window, the passer-by can admire twelve identical little girls, between thirteen and fourteen, pretty and shapely, more or less dressed in the successive items of the most expensive costume suggested for the great day, the first child in the row wearing only openwork black stockings with the chain and gold cross around her right thigh instead of a garter, the second having also pulled on the tight panties of bright red lace, all the way to the last entirely decked out in all her still immaculate veils. A few accessories of mortification hang among them, such as chains, cords, and whips. Inside, in order to give the children a taste for forgiveness and for sin, there are waxwork scenes, life-size, like the kind to be seen in police museums, but which here represent young saints at the most decorative moment of their martyrdom. Cut.

A problem arises. Who are the blond nurses, mentioned at varying intervals in the body of the text? What are they doing in the service of the psychoanalyst who employs them? What is their precise role in the narrative? Why have I written, in their regard, "false nurses"? And why are their white uniforms spattered with tiny red stains? Cut.

Retake. When Laura closes the library door behind her and turns around toward the big mirror, she notices on the black marble table top the skeleton key Ben-Saïd has forgotten. A remote smile passes like a shadow across her motionless face. With the slow movements of a sleepwalker, but without hesitations or breaks in continuity, she picks up the key, opens the door of her prison, neglecting to close it behind her, and walks down the straight street toward the subway station. Then it was certainly Laura whom I glimpsed from behind, pressed against the little rectangular window of the connecting door at the very end of the empty car I got into at the stop where I changed from the local to the express. A little later, as has been seen, she was captured by our agents who surrounded her on all sides: Ben-Saïd whose role consisted precisely in noting her flight and immediately warning the others, young W who is one of the three hoodlums encountered here and there in the narrative, Doctor Morgan himself, and M, The Subway Vampire. Cut.

Still later, Laura, who has been, during her entire interrogation, raped at great length and several times over by the two men, in various bizarre and uncomfortable postures which she has been forced to assume, which she has found very exciting after the nervous tension of her escape and the ambiguous pleasure caused by her own capture, is now imprisoned in the iron cage of the little underground room lined with white tiles. She has said disingenuous things to the surgeon on several occasions for the pleasure of lying, especially during the actual rapes. She recalls in particular the last confidences made at teatime by her brief companion Sarah Goldstücker, who seemed so eager to tell someone (whose mind she doubtless thought was shaky, which encouraged her to further outpourings, as she might have spoken to a deaf person or to a cat) the story of her dramatic youth: her eventful childhood, her difficulties during adolescence, the role of the sexually obsessed family doctor (whose name is not Müller, but Juard), etc. Cut.

Have I already indicated that even before the revolution, the entire city of New York, and in particular Manhattan Island, had been in ruins for a long time? I am speaking of course of the surface constructions, those in what is called the open air. One of the last houses still standing, the narrator's, located in the West Village, is now in the hands of a team of dynamiters. Having invoked the plan to construct soon, in its place, something higher and more modern, these four men with severe faces, dressed in dark gray sweatshirts, are skillfully and diligently planting all through the building their Bickford fuses and explosive charges, with a view to an explosion which cannot be long in coming now. Cut.

You have asked me what her ravishers did with the young bride. I can answer you in a few words. She figured for several days among the white slaves who are obliged to submit to services of all kinds—generally humiliating ones—at the will of members of the organization, in the conquered sections of the underground city. Then she was executed, on the pretext of some minor fault she committed during a ritual ceremony. They initially amused themselves by burning her with their cigars at the most sensitive and secret points of her body. They also forced her (at the same time and subsequently) to perform certain services of an intimate nature which the doomed girl was obliged to carry out to the best of her ability, despite her lack of experience. Finally they attached her arms and legs to the floor and wall of a cellar provided with huge rings set into the stone. When the body was stretched out in the shape of an X, arms and legs drawn wide apart by the chains fastened to her ankles and wrists, they stuck long needles into her flesh, especially through the breasts, in the buttocks, the thighs and the belly, in every direction and all the way through, from waist to knees, and they let her die that way. Cut.

I still had left to describe, in the same order of ideas, the fourth act of the torture of Joan, the pretty milky-skinned whore. But time is short. Soon it will be day. And now there has just appeared a "cat" somewhere in the sentence, apropos of Sarah the half-caste: a deaf man and a cat. The deaf man, I'm convinced, is the trumpet player at "Old Joe's." But the cat has not yet played any part here, to my knowledge; so that can only be a mistake . . . Apropos of the blond nurses and their incomprehensible presence in the organization, I should have found out, above all, what had become of the nicest one, that tall girl with the big dark glasses and the strong perfume, who kept brushing up against me . . . But it is too late. In the gray light of dawn, the hammering tread of the patrol is already echoing outside, at the very end of the long straight street where they advance, right down the middle of the pavement, with their calm, regular gait

. . . And Claudia . . . Who was Claudia? Why was she executed? . . . Yes, that's it, I was saying: with their calm, regular gait. The two militiamen are wearing navy-blue tunics and leather shoulder straps, with holsters over their hips; they are the same height, rather tall; they have faces that look alike—frozen, attentive, absent—under the flat-topped caps with very high front brims and the city emblem under it and a wide shiny visor which almost hides their eyes . . . And also: who is tapping in the blind room on the last floor, up at the very top of the big house? You're not going to try and make me believe it's old King Boris? . . . It sounds like pointed nails tapping against a door, or against a cast-iron radiator, as if someone were trying to send a message to other prisoners, especially women prisoners . . . And in that regard, just how did the second meeting go between JR and the mad old uncle who was not yet known as Goldstücker at the time? In any case I've already described—it will be remembered—how that exceptional girl had been recruited by means of a want ad, not one of the ones regularly published in *The New York Times* by so-called sophisticated couples who belong to the establishment, something like this: "Modern couple looking for weekend partners to play hearts. Photographs returned," which moreover we always answer systematically, sending the undressed picture of a handsome black man grinning with all his teeth and holding in his arms a delicate white-skinned creature, which has always obtained excellent results, but on the contrary by means of a text written this time by us, in order to encourage a more timid, not yet specialized clientele. A certain Jean Robertson, whom we subsequently renamed Joan, had answered the ad immediately, on the assumption she was dealing with some naïve businessman, someone easy to lure into a complicated affair, soon inextricably mixed up with stories of defective heroin and more or less consenting minors, which is to say rather less than more. From our first experiments, the call girl's remarkable gifts, in the various realms which interested the organization, had then saved her life (and this all the more easily in that she had claimed to be one of our own people, exhibiting a family passbook which was probably forged), until the day at least when N. G. Brown had discovered that the girl had just sold out to the local police. It remains possible of course that Brown lied in the report he turned over to Frank, and that he invented this betrayal out of whole cloth, having chosen the surest method of ridding himself for good of an inconvenient witness who might have given away his personal secrets: the presence in his house of the little captive removed from Doctor Morgan's menagerie, or even his own double game as an informer. Still, the fact is that the suspect had been sentenced to death without further trial . . . But, now that I think of it, one thing is certain: if the pink-and-blond complexion of the young nurses is not an artifice, they too must belong to the constantly renewed harem of war captives reduced to slavery. The little red stains, particularly numerous on the breast and from the hips to mid-thigh, would then be explained by the Pravaz needles which Doctor Morgan injects deep into their bodies through the white uniform (under which the reprieved victims generally wear nothing at all) in order to punish them for their daily delinquencies, the long hollow needles then having to remain planted in their flesh until the end of their night duty, even—or especially—if they make certain postures, certain attitudes, certain positions, or certain gestures extremely painful, which must in no case alter the professional smile enforced upon these creatures. (It has been shown, in particular, that the psychoanalyst prostitutes them to his paying customers whose sexual behavior he then studies by the direct experimental method.) The blood which trickles drop by drop through each slender steel channel . . . The cadenced sound of boots comes closer, and the regular rubbing of the holster against the leather belts, and the two black figures reflected in a gleaming double on the asphalt drenched by the recent shower . . . Faster, please, faster! And now, for the last act, Joan's splendid bloodstained body is lying on its back, head down, on the altar steps of an abandoned church in the depths of Harlem which has been used for a long time for expiatory ceremonies, but the blind organist keeps coming to play every day, so that the victims' screams can be drowned out by the uproar of the liturgical cadences. Moreover it is not impossible that the musician is also deaf, and that he is the one who plays the trumpet every night at "Old Joe's." The church in question has preserved all its old splendors: elaborate ornaments on every confessional and over each side chapel, huge black draperies which seem to smother the worshiper in the smoke of incense burners, gigantic carved motifs imitating the baroque where, among the arabesques, the billows, the scallops, the volutes, the scrolls, the garlands, appear the god of wrath, the god of the lightning, the god of tempests, each brandishing his attributes, the herald angels sounding their long trumpets, the mutilated corpses rising from their graves. Only the paving in the nave and the six steps of the high altar are of plain white marble. Here, surrounding the victim lying head down, legs wide apart, her feet attached to two giant candelabra which illuminate the scene with their countless tapers, the twelve still-virginal communicants in all their finery are kneeling, six on each side, on the marble steps, each one holding a lit black candle between hands fettered by a rosary instead of a chain. For an hour they have heard nothing but the religious music whose rolling waves break from the top of the vaults, occasionally resembling cries of mystic fervor; and they see nothing of the spectacle which is taking place ten feet away from them, because of the black bandages over their eyes, so that they still believe they are attending the high mass of their initiation, which remains true, in a sense. But in front of the twelve columns of the nave are already standing the twelve crosses to which the little girls are ultimately doomed: three crosses in the shape of an X, three in the shape of a T, three in the shape of a Y, three in the shape of an inverted Y. And beneath their blind gaze, the victim of the sacrifice lies in a pool of blood, the breasts torn off as well as all the flesh in the pubic area and the upper part of the thighs. Her delicate hands, carefully washed and very white, seem to caress these lacerations, in the hollow of the dark red wound which replaces the genitals; but these hands with their tapering fingers are like alien hands which are no longer attached to the body, for the arms too have been torn off and the blood which has gushed from the armpits has collected all around the head with its ecstatic smile resting on the slabs, the mouth and the eyes wide open, coagulating in the auburn hair spread out in cunning disarray, extending the curling locks in a flaming sun, like a scarlet octopus. But this time, I no longer have a minute to lose. I must return to that delicate girl who is still languishing in her cage, for M, The Vampire, and Doctor Morgan are now returning to the little white room in order to continue the interrogation, after having gone out for a sandwich to the drugstore in the nearby station. They remain standing, the two of them, in the room. They seem uncertain, exhausted. M pulls off his mask for a moment, with a mechanical gesture, trying to rub away, with the back of his hand, the wrinkles of his own face underneath; and Morgan, who then looks up from the papers accumulated on the table, recognizes with amazement the narrator's features. Without hesitating, realizing I have been discovered . . . Cut.

And suddenly the action resumes, without warning, and it is the same scene which proceeds all over again, very fast, always just as it was before. I have wrapped the girl in a blanket, as though to save her from the flames, climbing down the zigzag fire escape attached to a dizzyingly high building, where already the fire is roaring from roof to cellar. In the iron cage, padlocked once again, I have left in her place the slender skeleton of the other girl—the one the German television company did not want—whose bones are so neatly nibbled, so clean, so white, so varnished, that they seem to be made out of some plastic substance. And now I am closing the door behind me, after having set my precious burden down on the vestibule floor, while the police patrol stops to speak to the sentry on duty, in the recess of the house across the street, and now I am closing the door behind me, a heavy wooden door with a tiny narrow rectangular window in the top part, its pane protected by a . . . Cut. It is at this moment that I heard again the faint taps of a light hand, at the very top of the huge staircase of the enormous empty building, on a shaft of the central heating system. Laura has immediately raised her head, ears cocked, eyes fixed, lips pursed, as has already been said.

Selected Grove Press Paperbacks

E208	GENET, JEAN / The Blacks: A Clown Show / $2.95
B382	GENET, JEAN / Querelle / $2.95
B306	HERNTON, CALVIN C. / Sex and Racism in America / $2.95
E101	IONESCO, EUGENE / Four Plays (The Bald Soprano, The Lesson, The Chairs, and Jack, or The Submission) / $2.95
E259	IONESCO, EUGENE / Rhinoceros and Other Plays / $1.95
E216	KEENE, DONALD (Ed.) / Anthology of Japanese Literature; From the Earliest Era to the Mid-Nineteenth Century / $4.95
E573	KEENE, DONALD (Ed.) / Modern Japanese Literature / $5.95
B300	KEROUAC, JACK / The Subterraneans / $1.50
B9	LAWRENCE, D. H. / Lady Chatterley's Lover / $1.95
B373	LUCAS, GEORGE / American Graffiti / $1.50
B146	MALCOM X / The Autobiography of Malcolm X / $1.95
B326	MILLER, HENRY / Nexus / $2.95
B100	MILLER, HENRY / Plexus / $2.95
B325	MILLER, HENRY / Sexus / $3.95
B10	MILLER, HENRY / Tropic of Cancer / $1.95
B59	MILLER, HENRY / Tropic of Capricorn / $1.95
E636	NERUDA, PABLO / Five Decades: Poems 1925-1970 / $5.95
E359	PAZ, OCTAVIO / The Labyrinth of Solitude: Life and Thought in Mexico / $3.95
E315	PINTER, HAROLD / The Birthday Party and The Room / $2.95
E411	PINTER, HAROLD / The Homecoming / $1.95
B202	REAGE, PAULINE / The Story of O / $1.95
B323	SCHUTZ, WILLIAM C. / Joy / $1.95
B313	SELBY, HUBERT JR. / Last Exit to Brooklyn / $1.95
E618	SNOW, EDGAR / Red Star Over China / $4.95
B319	STOPPARD, TOM / Rosencrantz and Guildenstern Are Dead / $1.95
E219	WATTS, ALAN W. / The Spirit of Zen: A Way of Life, Work and Art in the Far East / $2.95

GROVE PRESS, INC., 196 West Houston St., New York, N.Y. 10014